Time Traveller

Jamie Tate

D0807759

Time Traveller

Jamie Tate

Vysian Banyard

Seven Arches
Publishing

Published in 2012
By Seven Arches Publishing
27, Church Street, Nassington, Peterborough PE8 61QG
www.sevenarchespublishing.co.uk

A catalogue record for this book is available from the British Library.

Cover design, scans and typesetting by Alan McGlynn.

Printed in Great Britain

ISBN 978-0-9567572-0-3

For Mum and Dad

‹IF THIS IS THE FIRST TIME YOU HAVE READ ONE OF THE BOOKS THAT RECORDS THE ADVENTURES OF CHILDREN FROM THE TWENTY FIRST CENTURY IN A TIMEZONE DIFFERENT TO TODAY. YOU NEED TO KNOW›

> That SHARP stands for The Scientific History and Art Reclamation Programme.

> That STRAP stands for the Scientific Testing and Recording of Aggression Programme.

> That time slip is something that you might suffer if you travel through time and space, in a similar way to how some people get jet lag when they fly long distances on a jet air liner.

> That if you travel through time and space you are a xrosmonaut.

CHAPTER 1

The History Lesson

'Jamie Tate!'

The teacher's voice cut across the quiet chatter in the classroom, making everybody sit bolt upright, everybody that is except Jamie himself, who was busy watching a tractor in the distance baling a field of hay. He was fascinated by the way that the machine gathered in great swathes of cut grass as it moved across the field, then stopped for a moment, whirred and clanked before shooting backwards and ejecting a large round bale of hay. He'd seen it so many times but it always made him want to laugh; he'd made his dad laugh by telling him it looked like a chicken laying an enormous egg.

'Jamie, did you hear me?' Mrs. Taylor's voice was louder now, some of the class began to giggle and there was a nudge here and there.

'It's no good, Miss, Jamie never listens,' piped up Adam Carter.

'He's miles away as usual,' said Caroline. 'Just like he always is, Miss.'

'Is Jamie actually here today, Miss?' came Nick's sarcastic voice, while his mates turned and smirked in Jamie's direction.

'Silence!' snapped Mrs. Taylor, only too aware that the class were mimicking the very things that she said repeatedly to Jamie Tate.

'Be quiet all of you please, and get on with your work.' Heads down, scribbling furiously, everyone waited for the thing that always came next.

'Jamie Tate, come here please... now!'

He heard her that time and dragged his attention away from the tractor in the distance.

His friend, Max, who was sitting next to him, nudged him in the ribs. Slowly Jamie got out of his chair and headed towards the front of the class. Mrs. Taylor drew herself up to her full height so that she was taller than the boy who stood in front of her with his head down, his toes wriggling nervously inside his shoes.

'Jamie, do you know what lesson this is?'

'Yes Miss, it's history.'

'But exactly *what* history, Jamie, are we studying this term?'

'The Romans, Miss.'

'And exactly what about the Romans?'

Now Jamie was stuck. He didn't have a clue. Vaguely he remembered hearing about an invasion of somewhere, a battle here, an emperor there, but beyond that...

'Well Jamie, I'm waiting.'

'Er, I don't know Miss.' Jamie looked up at the teacher, who was trying hard to control her frustration.

'Do you ever listen to a single thing I say? How can I teach you anything if you won't pay attention? What am I to do with you?'

At the back of the class someone said, 'Give up, Miss?' and the rest of the class burst out laughing, while Jamie stood at the front trying hard not to join in. He liked Mrs. Taylor and didn't want to upset her, but he hated history (not that there were any lessons that he did like).

Mrs. Taylor carried on speaking, trying to keep her voice calm. 'Please come and see me at break time, I shall be in the staff room. Now go and sit down and do your best to pay some attention!'

Jamie went back to his place and sat down, aware of Mrs. Taylor's gaze on him all the way. Everyone else was quiet, but he knew that they were watching him all the way back to his seat. A couple of kids gave him a wink and grinned as he went past.

'Right class 3T, think back to what we talked about last week. What can you remember?'

A dozen hands all shot up at once. The teacher surveyed the class.

'Well Anna, perhaps you would like to tell us.'

'Yes Miss,' said Anna brightly. Turning to Jamie with a smug look she said, 'We were talking about Roman Colchester and the revolt of Queen Boudica.'

'Well done Anna,' said Mrs. Taylor. How exciting it is that our own town, Colchester, was at one time the capital of Roman Britain. Who can remember what it was called?'

Jamie tried hard to think. Perhaps if he could answer a question, Mrs. Taylor might let him off staying in at break time. But it was no good; his mind was a complete blank.

Next to him Max had his hand up as high as he could get it and was frantically wiggling the tips of his fingers to try and get the teacher's attention.

'Go on Max,' said Mrs Taylor. 'You tell us.'

'Well Miss, it was called Colonia Claudia Victricensis, which means the Claudian Colony of the Victorious. It was called that because, at the time, it was the capital of Roman Britain and it was the Emperor Claudius who ordered the invasion.'

'An excellent answer, Max. You get a house point for that.'

Jamie felt a strong urge to pull a face at his friend for being such a know-it-all, but he didn't. Max loved history, which was incomprehensible. How could anyone love history? Jamie considered it to be just pointless stories.

Not to be outdone, Sarah piped up.

'And before the Romans came it was called Camulodunum, the fortress of Camulos the war god. It was a really important town even then.'

'Well done, Sarah, another brilliant answer. Now I'd like you all to work in pairs and use the laptops to follow the links I've set up. See what you can find out about the Roman invasion in AD 43. Am I right about that date?'

'Yes Mrs. Taylor,' chorused the class, including Jamie. He actually didn't know if that was the correct date, but because the others seemed to think so, that was good enough for him.

He tried to pay more attention for the rest of the lesson and Mrs.Taylor did notice, but it didn't stop her giving him a long lecture during break time about how rude it was not to pay attention and how he was wasting everyone's time, including his own, because he just didn't want to use his brain.

'I am sure your parents were not happy when they saw your half-term report, were they?'

Jamie didn't answer because the truth was they hadn't seen it. It was not that he had deliberately not given it to them, he had just forgotten. The report, along with a great many other letters from the school, was still in his school bag.

'You're letting them, and yourself, down.' Mrs. Taylor went on. 'Think about that, Jamie. I know how much you want to be a farmer when you leave school, just like your dad, but to get in to agricultural college you need to work really hard to pass your exams. I know you have a good brain in there somewhere – just use it!'

But Jamie had heard it all before.

'What's got to you at school today?' asked Dan, Jamie's older brother, as they got off the school bus that evening and started the half-mile walk together down the small lane to the farm.

'Nothing,' mumbled Jamie.

'Had a bad day?' Dan wasn't giving up, but at least he didn't add 'again', even though that was what he was thinking. He knew only too well that his brother usually had a bad time in school. It was odd, Dan was just two years older than Jamie and they were very similar in many ways, but he enjoyed school; lessons seemed easy to him. He had done well from the day he had started in nursery school, and he still did well. His ambition was to get to university and study law, and he knew that everyone expected him to pass the exams he needed. For his brother, it seemed so different. Of course, Jamie couldn't understand how Dan found everything so easy. But they were good mates. Jamie always felt Dan was on his side, whatever.

'Hey, when we get home, what about we have a game of Call of Duty?'

'Thanks, Dan, that'll be great!' For the first time that day Jamie cheered up. But if he thought he'd had a hard day at school, worse was to come when he got home.

CHAPTER 2

The School Report

When they got to the farm, almost before he had time to get through the door, Jamie's mother started on a long lecture about not emptying his school bag.

'Just sit down at the table, James, while I check what's in your bag,' she said, while Dan gave a grin and escaped upstairs to his room.

Their gran, who was sitting on the other side of the table with one of her amazing fruit cakes in front of her, gave Jamie an encouraging smile, but that didn't make up for the tight frown on his mother's face.

'Just look at this lot in here,' his mother said as she shook his bag open on the table. Out came an assortment of old sandwich wrappers, half-eaten apples, orange peel, his battered pencil case and numerous pens that didn't work. Finally, a flutter of school letters, informing his parents of school events, no doubt long since past, fell out in an untidy pile.

'You can just sit there and wait now until I've looked through all these letters. How many times have I told you to give them to me on the day you get them?'

'But Mum,' Jamie pleaded, ' Dan said he would give me a game before he starts his homework.'

'Well, we'll see about that. First I'm going to read through all these letters I should have received over the last few weeks. And whose fault is it that I haven't seen them? I'm much too busy with the Bed and Breakfast customers to be searching through the school bag of a twelve-year-old!'

Wow, thought James. She's well miffed.

'Sorry, Mum,' he muttered, beginning to feel ashamed that he was adding to his mum's workload. He knew how hard it was for her to keep the B and B and the farm shop going, which in turn helped the farm to make money.

'But do you really want to be bothered, reading all that stuff?'

'Yes, James, I do, and it would be much better if you did as well,' answered his mother. He sat still and said nothing for a while. Then his gran cut him a slice of the fruitcake. She slid the slice onto a plate and pushed it across towards him. Jamie gave her a grateful smile, and took a huge bite.

'And look at this one. It says your class is going on a school trip to Colchester Castle next week. You have to take ten pounds in by…goodness me, it's by tomorrow. Look at that now. If I hadn't looked in your bag and read all these letters, you'd have missed the trip. You do want to go, don't you?'

'Yes, I suppose I do,' he mumbled through a mouthful of cake. 'I don't want to be the only one not going. Everyone's really keen about it. Honestly, Mum, I really meant to ask you at the week-end but I forgot, what with going up the top field to help dad move the electric fencing. I just forgot all about it. I'm sorry.'

'Jamie, it's great you like helping your dad, but school must come first.'

Just as Mrs. Tate said those words, the back door opened and Mr. Tate came in. He'd been busy on the farm since early in the morning and he looked tired.

'What's that I'm hearing?' said Mr. Tate, his expression changing from a hearty smile to a frown that matched his wife's.

'I've just been telling Jamie that he must make sure he gives us all the letters from school. Look at this lot – some of it is weeks old!'

Jamie's dad sorted through the crumpled pile of papers on the table. He picked up one particularly creased brown envelope and opened it slowly.

'What's this, Jamie?'

Oh, oh, thought Jamie. I'm really in for it now. It was that half-term report, which Mrs. Taylor had asked him about that afternoon. The one he had been given a week ago and promptly forgotten all about. It certainly wasn't going to contain good news.

'This is your school report, Jamie,' said his dad, quickly scanning the page. As he did so his frown became deeper, the lines etching his weather-beaten face.

'Do you know what this says?'

'Er... no dad, we're not supposed to open it.'

Jamie's mum took the paper from her husband and read it carefully. Jamie glanced towards his gran for help. She gave him a quick smile, but got up and went over to the sink, making a big show of washing up a few cups; she didn't want to be involved.

'Jamie, this is not good,' said his mum. She paused and heavy silence filled the room. 'It's not good at all. The teachers all say the same: that you don't listen or pay attention in class. Am I right in thinking we've seen all this before?'

Jamie stared down at the table. He felt himself go red to the tips of his ears. He hated upsetting his parents, and he'd really done it now.

Mr. Tate spoke sternly in a voice you didn't dare

argue with.

'Go upstairs to your room please, and don't come down until I tell you to. Your mum and I need to have a good look at this.'

'Yes dad,' he mumbled. He couldn't wait to get out of the room.

It was late in the evening and the farmhouse was silent, except for the quiet ticking of the old grandfather clock in the corner of the sitting room. The clock had been there for so long that no one knew where it had first come from. Both boys had gone to bed, and Gran had taken herself off to watch the television in her own room. Mr. and Mrs. Tate were sitting in the armchairs in front of the glowing log fire. Doodles, Jamie's dog, lay on the mat, her feet twitching furiously as she dreamt of chasing rabbits through the woods. Mr. Tate was still frowning.

'Hazel, this has gone far enough. I've tried to be patient with Jamie but this school report has to be the worst one so far. It's terrible. No, it's far worse than that!'

Jamie's mum nodded sadly. It had been so awful, she had found it hard to take in. Every teacher had said what a nice, polite boy Jamie was, she had smiled when she read that, but the rest was just dreadful, and it was all the same. Jamie never paid attention, never listened, never took anything in. It was as if there was no point in him being there at all, although none of the teachers had actually said that. Every grade for every subject, apart from PE, was the lowest you could get. Yes, something had to be done, but what? They were perplexed. They had always tried to support the school, attended parents' evenings and gone in to see the teachers when they had been asked to. They had spoken to Jamie, reasoned with him, got mad with him, bribed him, tried everything, and so had Gran, but so far nothing had worked. Getting angry was no good; Jamie just switched off. Something had to be done. They had to come up with a plan, and come up with one fast!

It was late by the time they finally went upstairs to bed. For some hours they had sat by the fire, watching the logs burn down to glowing embers, tossing ideas this way and that. And at last they had come up with something, something they hadn't tried before. They didn't like it, but now they had a plan, and surely it would work, or so they hoped.

The next day was a Saturday. Jamie and Dan

spent the morning with their dad, fixing one of the drains in the cattle yard, which had somehow got blocked. It was a dirty, smelly job and had kept them all busy for some time. When they were finished, put everything away and had cleaned themselves up, Dan said he had better get going. He was meeting a couple of mates in town.

Mr Tate asked Jamie to come and give him a hand in the farm office. Jamie was surprised. Normally his dad didn't like him going in there. Jamie went and sat next to his dad and watched him working on the computer. He wasn't interested much in what was on the screen, but he liked being there. He felt important being allowed into the office. As far as he knew, Dan, who was much better on the computer than he was, had never been asked to help out in the office, although their mum often did, working on the farm accounts.

'Well,' said his dad, suddenly looking very serious. 'The farm made a good profit last year. We're getting a fair price for the beef cattle and putting more land down to wheat was a sensible thing to do.' There was a pause. Jamie wondered if his dad expected him to say something.

'Yes, your great-great-great-grandparents would

have been proud. The farm has been in our family all that time, Jamie. It was just a few acres when the first Tate's bought it, but they worked hard and expanded it, and my dad and his dad and his dad before him did the same. They'd hardly recognise it now, but they'd be proud of what this family has done.'

'Yes, Dad, you're right,' said Jamie, watching the swallows dart in and out of the rafters above the stables. 'It's a great farm.'

'Been in this family all those generations,' went on Mr. Tate, almost as if he'd forgotten Jamie and was talking to himself. 'We've built it up so well. It will be a shame to sell it.'

'Sell it?' Jamie's attention was suddenly caught. He was no longer watching the swallows. Sell the farm? That couldn't be right! The farm should pass to him, as it had for generations, from father to son. What did Dad mean? He couldn't sell the farm!

Mr. Tate kept speaking as if he hadn't heard Jamie or seen his son's shocked face.

'Farming isn't like it used to be, you know. When my dad was here it was all about hard, physical work, grafting in all weathers, doing what you could, whatever got thrown at you. If the tractor went wrong you got out the spanner, but now you have to fix the computer first. To run a farm now you need to be an accountant, solicitor, stock controller, businessman, IT expert. You name it, that's what farmers have to be nowadays. It's hard work, exacting work and mistakes can cost you dear.'

For a few minutes Mr. Tate stopped talking. He stared into the distance, as if he were seeing things as they used to be, in the days when he took over the running of the farm from his father. Then suddenly he sat up straight and stared intently at the computer screen again. There was a long silence, broken only by the crowing of a cockerel out in the farmyard.

Jamie's mind was reeling from what his dad had said to him. Was he really thinking of selling the farm? Why would he want to do that?

'Dad...' he paused, almost too afraid to ask anything more. 'What do you mean, sell the farm? You can't do that. When you give up, I'll take over – you know that's what will happen. It's always been like that.'

Mr. Tate turned and looked hard at his son.

'Jamie, I know you love this farm, but if you can't run it properly, deal with all the business side of it, keep it going as it should be run, if you can't do that, I'd rather sell it. And maybe I should sell it before your mum and I wear ourselves out completely. Land prices are very high right now; they might not always stay like that.'

'Dad, you know I will do my best to run the farm properly. I'll go to agricultural college, get a degree, anything, just don't sell the farm!'

'Will you? Will you get to college? You don't seem to be making any effort to achieve that.' Mr. Tate sighed heavily. 'Jamie, your brother doesn't want the farm. He wants to go to university and get a high-flying job in the city. He knows what he wants, and he's working hard towards it. You know what you want too, but you won't put in the work to get it. Your mum and I have made up our minds. Whoever gets this farm when we're gone has got to keep it going successfully, expand it, make it grow. If you can't do that, we'll sell it to someone who can.'

Jamie could hardly believe what he was hearing, but he could see from the look on his father's face that he meant every word he said. He had a terrible feeling in the pit of his stomach. It felt as if his whole world had been turned upside down. He tried to say something, but the right words wouldn't form in his head. The office door opened and his mum came in.

'Dinner's ready,' she said, and then saw the look

on Jamie's face. She caught her husband's eye and he gave her a slow wink. She knew what that meant – the plan was now in place. As Jamie left the office and walked slowly across the yard, his shoulders hunched and his head low, she asked her husband, 'Has it worked? Did he listen?'

'Yes, he listened, alright. It's given him a real jolt. Time will tell, though. He's just had the shock of his life. Now we'll have to wait and see what he decides to do.'

After lunch, Jamie escaped outside with Doodles. He hadn't felt like eating. As he walked away from the house, his legs seemed to be moving on their own. He had no idea where he was going. He went over and over in his head what his dad had said. Surely, surely, they wouldn't sell the farm? They worked hard, very hard. They hardly ever had a holiday; perhaps they had just had enough? If they sold it, they would have enough money to live comfortably without all that work. But he couldn't bear the idea of someone else having the place. It was just too awful to think about, but he knew his dad was right; farms had to move with the times in order to make enough money. But why did his parents have so little faith in him? He didn't mind hard work, except the sort of work you did at school. Of course, it was that school report that had done it. Somehow, he would have to try to improve his grades. He'd have to show them he could do it, prove to them that he could work to get what he wanted.

CHAPTER 3

A Visitor From The Future

Despite Jamie's determination to work harder at school, it wasn't that easy. Teachers seemed to ignore him half the time, as if they had already given up on him. He tried hard to listen and follow what they were saying, but he had let himself slip so far behind, half the time he had no idea what they were talking about. He picked up a little in maths. When they were doing some work on turning decimals into fractions, he found himself actually understanding Mr Butler's quick explanation on the whiteboard, and he got his first answer right and a brief, and surprised, 'well done' from Mr. Butler. But at other times, he began to wonder if he was just stupid. Was he too thick to do well? He had never been so miserable in all his life.

The weekend before the school trip, he decided he would go down to the pond in the woods to check if the frogspawn had hatched. Last year there had been loads; he had always liked finding the blobs of grey jelly floating just under the water in the pond, and then going back a week or two later to check to see if any tadpoles had hatched. He still felt as if a dark cloud of misery followed him wherever he went, but being outdoors was not as bad as indoors. He wandered through the woods with Doodles following at his heels, until he reached the pond. It was surrounded by tall reeds, except for one place where the earth had been flattened, providing an ideal spot to kneel down and peer into the water. It was a bright, sunny day and his reflection stared back at him from deep inside the pond. At first Doodles crashed around in the undergrowth, following the scent of animals only he knew about, but then he came and lay down beside him.

Jamie was engrossed, and time slipped away. He watched the tiny froglets darting here and there in the clear water, and became oblivious to everything except the little creatures in their underwater world. But suddenly he was jerked back to reality by the loud and insistent ringing of his mobile, stuffed deep in his jacket pocket. He fumbled for it, digging about amongst old conkers, bits of string and other rubbish. At last he pulled it out and sat scowling at it. The ringing had stopped, but there was a strange blue haze on the screen, and try as he might he couldn't do anything with it, and it didn't even show a missed call, just a weird swirling blue mist on the screen.

Blast, thought Jamie – was it broken? He remembered how his phone had been in his pocket when he fell in the brook, up to his waist, in water a few days earlier. He'd been trying to straighten one of the stepping stones and slipped on the wet weed. Maybe a good soaking had done something awful to it? But, then, if it was broken, why had it just rung? He stuffed it back into his pocket and lay down to peer again into the depths of the pond.

The warmth of the sun beat down on his back and he began to feel drowsy. Suddenly there was another reflection staring back at him. Another boy was looking down into the pond too. He jerked wide-awake and swung round. Doodles had let someone creep up on him! He hadn't let out even the smallest of growls and now the dog was staring at the intruder as if he had known him all his life: that was seriously peculiar. Doodles was a very good guard dog.

'Who are you? Why did you creep up on me like that?'

'Hello Jamie,' said the boy, not answering his questions.

How come this boy knew his name!? The stranger was about his own size, with smooth brown hair and a freckled face. He was wearing clothes just like his except that they were remarkably clean. But it was the boy's eyes that caught his attention, they were bright and deep blue, just like the blue mist on his mobile.

'Who are you?' Jamie repeated.

The boy smiled and sat back, staring at Jamie.

'I've been looking for you, Jamie,' he said. 'My name's Leika. Listen, I haven't much time and there's a lot to explain. Look at me.'

Unable to stop himself, Jamie looked into the strange boy's eyes. He felt himself go faint and a bit dizzy. The world seemed to swoop and dive all around him, and then it began to settle and he felt as if somehow he knew everything there was to know about the countryside around him and the animals that lived in it, as if he had become a part of it all himself. For a moment he felt as if his head would explode with all the new knowledge that had been forced into it in one split second. He felt as if his limbs had become the branches of a tree, and his hair its leaves rustling in the breeze. He became the water flowing over the stones in the stream and the birds swooping and darting high in the sky. For a few brief moments he became the world around him, and it surged and pulsed inside his brain and made his head pound wildly. Then, just as he felt he could bear it no longer, everything steadied. Jamie leaned forward, gasping out loud. When he looked at the boy called Leika again, he saw that he was still smiling at him.

'Hey, you did that to me, didn't you!'

'Yes I did. We know how much nature means to you, so we thought we'd help you to understand it better.'

For some reason Jamie didn't feel surprised that he had said 'we' instead of 'I'.

'Listen,' Leika carried on. 'We picked you to do a job for us. It will be hard for you to understand, but I come from the future, from a time in your future.' He was speaking slowly, as if to give Jamie time to understand the things he was saying. 'I have come because we need you to go back into the past for us. I, and the others who come from my time, can't usually go back further than this, past the twenty-first century, but you can.'

Jamie's mind was whirling, thoughts and questions darting everywhere. His day watching tadpoles was turning into something very different.

'I... I don't understand.'

The boy went on, all the time staring deep into Jamie's eyes as if he would pierce his very brain.

'As I have just said, I come from far in the future. I belong to an organisation called SHARP. Those letters stands for the Scientific History and Art Reclamation Programme. Our job is to find out the history of past times. Things happened in the world after your time that weren't good. We call that the time of Dark Chaos. There was conflict across the globe, disease and changing weather that became more and more catastrophic, and as a result all historical records were lost.'

Jamie felt a cold shiver of fear.

'Did…did people survive?'

'Oh yes, people survived, but it was a bad, bad time and destruction was massive. A few very good scientists managed to preserve knowledge and to build a world civilisation again but there are no different countries or peoples; we are just humankind. We are trying to piece things together from the past by sending travellers back in time, but we can't do it by ourselves because, as I have just explained, going back as far as the twenty-first century is our limit. I've been chosen to ask you, Jamie, if you'll travel back in time for us. Will you be a SHARP agent?'

Jamie looked at Leika blankly. This was way too much for him to take in.

'Does it scare you?' Leika asked.

Jamie shook his head in a conscious effort to clear his mind.

'No, of course not. But why choose me? I hate history, I'm rubbish at...'

'Don't worry, we know how badly you're doing at school but I chose you, Jamie, because I know how much the natural world means to you. You care for the world and the creatures in it. I also chose you because you hate school.' He laughed. 'I chose you Jamie be-cause you remind me of what I was like at your age. I hated school too, but then I found out that I could re-ally help the animals and plants, the world around me, if I worked hard at lessons. Now I have a university doctorate in Natural Sciences and with the time travel project, we are achieving a great deal in nature con-servation. We can ensure that species of both flora and fauna are saved from extinction.'

'But you're not old enough to have studied to university level. You can't be any older than I am!'

'Ah Jamie, when you travel in time, things can be deceptive. I'm much older than I look. For example, when you travel back in time you might think you've been away for ages but in fact it'll only be a few min-utes in your actual time. I need to ask you again, will you become a SHARP agent?'

Jamie didn't know what to say. His mind was reeling, but no matter how ridiculous it might sound, the thought of being able to travel back in time was amazing, it was totally, totally cool. And these people called SHARP had chosen him, surely he can't be that stupid if they had done that?

'How do I get to travel back in time, and where am I going?'

'Do you remember that your mobile rang just before I arrived?'

Jamie nodded, reaching into his pocket.

'Get it out and look at it. It was SHARP getting in touch with you.'

Jamie pulled out his mobile and stared at it. Somehow it looked different, and with a start he realised that three extra app icons had appeared on the screen.

'The three different apps, all with a phoenix to distinguish them, have been put there by SHARP. When you're on your own and you're sure you won't be disturbed, press the black phoenix app and it will give you all the information you need to know. The other two, the red phoenix and the green one will be explained to you at a later time. You've been chosen,

Jamie. You will be on SHARP's Time Traveller programme. Now, remember this number,16008. It's your unique number. And don't forget my name, I'm your contact person at SHARP.'

As Leika had been speaking, his voice became fainter and fainter and finally faded out altogether. A blue mist swirled in front of Jamie's eyes. He was standing alone by the pond, his mobile held in his hand, and there was no sign of Leika.

Jamie could hardly wait for tea to finish that night. He didn't eat his usual massive portion, but this didn't surprise anyone that much. Although his appetite had begun to pick up after his shock about the possibility of selling the farm the previous week, he had not really returned to his old self and his parents had been on what Dan called 'worry watch'.

'Are you OK Jamie?' asked his mum, kindness and concern in her voice. 'Don't forget it's your school trip to Colchester Castle tomorrow. I hope you're not coming down with something – it would be a shame to miss it.'

'No mum, I'm fine,' said Jamie. 'I'm just a bit tired. I might go to bed early.'

'Ooh shock horror news item: Jamie Tate doesn't

eat all his usual super-sized-gigantic-tea,' said Dan, grinning wickedly.

'Dan,' said his mother. 'Stop teasing.'

'Aye Dan, give over,' said Mr. Tate, looking up from his newspaper for an instant.

'Well you should be pleased, the two of you, that Jamie's started to get the message that eating enough for at least three normal people might just cause him health problems in later life.'

No one was more surprised than Dan when Jamie didn't give back as good as he got.

He just stared at Dan in a vacant way and then got up from the table and said. 'Good night everyone, I'm going to get an early night before the trip tomorrow.'

CHAPTER 4

Time Travel Instructions

As soon as he escaped to his own room, Jamie pulled out his mobile, put it on the table and stared at the screen. The new app beckoned, and he reached out his finger towards the black outline of a phoenix bird. But he didn't press it; his finger stopped, hovering in mid-air. He thought of his strange meeting with Leika. Did he really want to do this? Could Leika be trusted? But if he didn't press it, he'd never find out what was involved. After all, if he didn't like what he saw, he could always pull out. He leaned forward and impulsively jabbed his finger on the app… and waited.

For a moment nothing happened, and then the screen flickered into life. Words began to appear, and Jamie read rapidly. As he did so the screen scrolled down and the message continued.

Jamie, thank you for getting in touch with SHARP. We will tell you more about our method of time travel, but first a word of caution. Time travel is not a new concept for SHARP and we have successfully sent a number of people back into the past and retrieved them safely. But there will always be an element of risk and we cannot fully guarantee your return. It is important that you understand this. If you do not feel comfortable about it, you can withdraw now and we will understand completely.

For a second, and only for a second, Jamie hesitated, and then he felt a sudden surge of excitement. Withdraw? I don't think so. He couldn't withdraw now. He went on reading.

Thank you for your confidence in us. SHARP is an organisation dedicated to finding out about the past history of the world we live in. We do this with the strict policy that we will do our best to ensure that neither our time travellers, nor the people they meet in the chosen time zone, will suffer any ill effects or danger from this operation. Our company's aim is to use the knowledge found to ensure a better future for the wonderful world we live in.

The screen cleared then a new message appeared.

We will provide you with full details of your time travel. The information will come to you from Leika, a fully authorised student of the University of SHARP. You have already met him and he will be your contact with us from now on. Once again, Jamie, we thank you for your willingness to help us. If you choose to become a SHARP agent your contribution will be of enormous benefit to all humankind.

The screen faded completely and for a moment Jamie thought he had lost contact. But suddenly it sprang into life again, a series of numbers flashing across it, almost too fast for him to follow. He blinked quickly and, as the numbers began to slow down, realised that it was counting down the years. It stopped at 2012, and another message appeared.

Hello Jamie, this is Leika. It was good to meet you, and I'm glad you've decided to find out more information about SHARP. What follows is the company's standard information on time travel.

Then the small screen on his phone seemed to detach itself and slowly enlarge into something like a television screen that hovered in front of his eyes.

Amongst the swirling colours on the screen was a message:

‹WELCOME, JAMIE TATE, TO SHARP 16008›

You can put the mobile phone down now and the new screen will stay in place until you touch the black phoenix again.

For a moment Jamie felt a sense of fear. This huge screen, all the messages; what was SHARP capable of and who were they? Well, there was only one way to find out. Jamie carefully put the mobile phone down and watched the screen as the message faded. The background of swirling colours became more intense than anything he had ever seen before, and then seemed to spin off the screen and into the air all around him. Jamie began to feel quite giddy but suddenly the screen cleared and the following text appeared.

This is an invitation to you to join our project. We have contacted you because we think you are particularly suited to Project 16008, but we will quite understand if after careful consideration you decline to take part.

Our company policy is: Be of good hope, and travel back in time and return in the spirit of greater good for all humankind.

Again the screen changed and another message appeared. This time it was Leika again.

‹INSTRUCTIONS to Jamie Tate from Leika›

Well Jamie, this is it. The instructions below come from me but they are standard SHARP instructions, as I have said before, that are given to all potential time travellers. Read them carefully, and if you have any questions you can text them to SHARP 16008.

‹Pre-travel information›

When there is the possibility of a journey to a different time zone, the screen of your mobile will glow blue and you will feel a low-level vibration, different in pulse to its usual one. This may last for up to two hours in your time. After that the opportunity will have passed.

‹Travel information›

If you are ready to travel, make sure you are alone and somewhere where you will not be interrupted for a while. When you are time travelling you will be gone for between **four and six minutes** of your time, but to you it will seem to be much longer. It is not desirable for anyone to see you go or return, so make sure that no one is likely to be worried by your disappearance. Wearing clothes is not helpful, so you will need to wear something skin tight – what you call swimming trunks is probably best. You will receive from us a small bag that you must wear. It doesn't need ties or anything. It is called a time/space bag. When you have taken your clothes off, press the bag to your waist, on top of any skin-tight item you are wearing. **Do this BEFORE you go**. The bag contains a small silver disc that you must put on your forehead when you arrive. The disc is invisible and almost weightless, so you will not notice it, but it will record everything you see as it contains what to you would be a camera. It only activates when it is worn, and only lasts a short while, so do not put it on until AFTER you arrive in the past. On your arrival, take the disc out and press it to your forehead. The backing disc will come away. If you are going back to a time and place where a different language is spoken there will be a special hearing aid that will fit perfectly into your ear. It will translate, without you realising it, what people are saying to you and the words you say to them will be translated as you speak. I repeat, you must press the time/space travel bag to your side for safe keeping. It attaches itself to you without any discomfort. It cannot be taken from you and assures your safe return. I was wearing one when I met you.

‹Getting Ready to Depart›
When you are ready to go, **press the black phoenix** and then **chose the number option** and **key in** your project number **16008**. A screen will appear that will tell you where you are going, what you will see and whom you will meet. It identifies a destination. Read these travel instructions very carefully, and when you are sure you have understood them, **key in** project number **16008** and then **press the green phoenix**. The system will be activated and you will be transported to the time zone indicated. Near to where you arrive there will be a pile of clothes suitable for the time and place. You must put these on as quickly as possible. By putting on these clothes you will take on the character and personality of the person you will become in the new time zone. That is why the people you meet will either mistake you for someone they know or will not be surprised that a stranger is amongst them. On your journeys you will find that you

can help people; this you should do. Never do anything unkind.

‹Return journey›

When it is time for you to return, you will feel the phone vibrating. You will have to take off the clothes and leave them in a pile, preferably somewhere they can-not be seen too easily. Take the phone out of the bag, **press the red phoenix** and **key in 16008**. If you need to return because of danger before the phone vi-brates, remove the clothes as described above and **just press the red phoenix**. This should only be done under real emergency conditions. Alternatively, if your return must be instantaneous, you may keep on your clothes but **only if there is extreme peril** as if may af-fect the working of the transporter to some degree.

‹After your visit›

We will contact you after your visit to give you an as-sessment of how well you have done.

So Jamie, that's the standard instructions, now all you have to do is wait. We will be sending you an option to travel in the next few days. If you do not take up this option for 11 is or the next two option times, we will assume that you have decided to decline our invitation, and we will return your mobile to its original state and retrieve our travel bag.

Finally the screen cleared, followed by the words:

Goodbye Jamie, we'll be in contact very soon.

And then it went blank. Putting the phone down carefully, Jamie leaned back on the pillow, suddenly feeling exhausted. So much information to take in, so much to think about! But he felt a huge excitement building up inside him, and he could hardly wait for the next message from SHARP. It would have information about where he was travelling to. Unbelievable!

CHAPTER 5

The Temple In The Vaults

Monday morning, and Jamie's class piled onto the coach, laughing and chattering. The teachers handed out clipboards to which a number of work-sheets were attached, and gave the customary lecture on how they expected everyone to behave while they were out of school. Jamie reached into his pocket and his hand closed around his mobile phone.

The first part of the morning was spent looking around Colchester Castle Museum itself; one after another of glass cases containing bits of pottery, old coins, statues and pots of ashes. Jamie tried hard to concentrate as he went around with Max, but after a while all the exhibits began to blur into each other and look the same. The display of Roman soldiers jerked him awake for a while, impressed by the weight of their mail tunics and their vicious looking swords. But after that, even though he tried hard to remember his vow to concentrate more, he felt his attention beginning to drift.

'Jamie! Did you hear what I said?' Mrs. Taylor's

voice cut across the fog in his mind. 'We're going to have a tour of the castle vaults now.'

Vaults? Ah yes, the vaults. As they'd gone into the castle that morning he'd seen the steps leading down, deep under the castle and into the very foundations of the Roman temple of Claudius. Max could hardly wait. He had said that it would be the best bit of the trip. Obediently, Jamie shuffled in behind the others and the guide unlocked the gate leading to the vaults. As she was doing so she pointed out a large mosaic showing two young boys fist fighting, and explained how it had been found in an excavation carried out in the town.

'We believe this mosaic must have come from a high-status household, possibly one of the town leaders.'

Jamie was impressed. It was a huge picture created by small rectangular pieces of coloured pottery. It must have taken whoever made it ages to put all the pieces of pot into the right places. At the top of the steps into the vaults the guide paused and then said dramatically, 'We're going back in time. Every step down is going back one hundred years in history.'

The guide's words rang in Jamie's head: 'going back in time'. Would SHARP contact him now? he wondered as he reached the bottom step and peered ahead into the gloom.

The children had to stoop down to pass under the thick, arched walls that separated the vaults. The floor underfoot was sandy and somehow muffled the sounds around them. When they reached the central vault, the guide began to explain how and why the temple was built, and how it had been destroyed by Boudica, Queen of the Iceni, who hated the Romans and what they had done to her people. Jamie listened intently for a while, but then something strange seemed to be happening. Standing in the centre of the vault was a shining, white model of the Roman Temple of Claudius, which had been built on the very spot where they were standing. As he stared at it he felt the graceful white columns rising up above him, their gold porticoes soaring into the sky. It seemed as if people pressed around him, his head pulsed and throbbed and the air was filled with the sound of strange chanting and the sweet smell of incense. Lights from oil lamps were dancing in front of his eyes. Jamie clutched at his neighbour as he felt himself swaying and his knees buckling.

'Oy, get off me Jamie,' said Adam Pitt, whose coat Jamie was clutching. 'What you doing?'

Jamie snapped back to the world around him and the model of the temple was just a model again. Then he felt his mobile start to vibrate. It was vibrating with the pulse that told him SHARP was getting in touch.

'Jamie,' Mrs. Taylor called out from across the group. 'Will you let go of Adam, now! What do you think you're playing at?'

Jamie's hand dropped to his side. He saw Max give him a concerned look.

'Sorry Miss,' he muttered. 'It's just… just I don't feel too good. It's really stuffy in here.' The colour had drained out of Jamie's cheeks and Mrs. Taylor suddenly looked worried. She went and stood beside him. Jamie felt embarrassed. The guide and the rest of the class were staring at him, but their faces seemed to be floating in some kind of a haze.

'Miss,' he mumbled. 'Can I go back up? I just need some fresh air.'

'Do you want me to come with you?' asked Max.

'No, no Max, honestly I'm fine. You don't want to miss what's going on here.'

Mrs. Taylor nodded at the guide, who took Jamie back up the steps and left him in the care of a kindly museum assistant in the first aid room.

'You sit there, lad and I'll get you a glass of water – you'll soon feel fine again.'

He was right. Jamie began to feel perfectly normal, once he had got back up the stairs from the vault. Now all he wanted to do was get out his phone and read SHARP's message. The museum assistant came back with the glass of water.

'You can stay here lad. Your class will finish their tour in about half an hour. I've got to go and help out in the shop. It's only over there, and no one can come in here without me seeing them. Give me a shout if you need anything.'

'Thanks, Sir,' said Jamie. 'Sorry to be a trouble, but is there a toilet?'

'The staff toilet's just through that door. It's OK you can use it.'

As soon as the man had gone, Jamie pulled out his mobile and stared at the screen. A message flashed up. It was SHARP!

He read it quickly. 'Directions for the journey' it said, and somehow that seemed so ordinary, as if he was catching a bus into the town centre to see his friends rather than about to take a step back into the unknown. It was so ludicrous that for a moment he almost laughed out loud, but then he read the message again, very carefully.

> Thank you again for agreeing to work with us. We hope you will enjoy your trip, although as we have said before it will involve some element of danger.

Yes, yes, thought Jamie. I know that, but I'm not afraid, although deep down he wasn't entirely sure who he was trying to kid.

The message went on.

> These are your detailed travel instructions. Please read them carefully and try to memorise them.

‹Time zone›
AD 60.

‹Place›
Roman Colchester.

‹Landing›
A small house in the precinct of the Temple of Claudius.

‹Instructions›
When you arrive you will find a pile of clothes lying

nearby. It is vital that you put them on immediately. As soon as you have done this, leave the room and wait by one of the colonnades. Someone will come to find you.

‹Identify›
Your name will be Marcus, and you are the servant to Flavius, one of the town's leading Roman citizens.

‹Conditions›
Local disturbances: unsure of how severe.

‹Equipment›
Mobile phone and travel bag with a camera disc and the hearing aid for language translation. If you feel in your coat pocket you will find the travel bag there. Remove all your clothes except your under pants and then press the travel bag against your side. It will stick firmly in place and cannot be dislodged. As soon as you are ready, **press the green phoenix** and **key in the number 16008**. Your journey will then begin. Remember to put the camera on your forehead and the language translation aid into your ear. Also remember, that to return you need to press the red phoenix. Good luck!

Jamie took several deep breaths to steady his nerves and stop his hands shaking. Up until now, in a strange way, he had felt as if the whole thing had been some kind of dream, and it wouldn't really happen. But now, he was on the verge of putting his own safety, his life, entirely in SHARP's hands and setting off on what could be an incredibly dangerous journey back into time. He pulled himself together. The whole thing was way too good to miss. For some reason that he couldn't explain, he felt sure that SHARP wouldn't let him down.

He pushed open the staff toilet door, went through and locked the door behind him. He felt in his pocket and sure enough there was the travel bag, which looked like a strong plastic bag with a velcro seal. It hadn't been there when he'd left home that morning. As he pulled off his clothes, leaving just his underpants on, his hands were now quite steady, and the travel bag seemed to melt into his side as he pushed it firmly with his fingers. Jamie pressed the green phoenix and then hesitated as the keyboard appeared. All he had to do now was the number. His hand trembled a little as he keyed in 16008. He just had time to think, 'Here goes!' before he heard a high pitched humming noise getting louder and louder. The world spun around him with the noise piercing into his head until it was almost unbearable and then... Nothing.

CHAPTER 6

A Temple In The Sun

Jamie landed on a cold stone floor. For a moment he gasped for breath, then sat up slowly as he felt things steadying around him. He was sitting on the floor of what appeared to be a tiny room, with a small window high up in one corner. Weak sunlight filtered through and left a shaft of light shining on the floor. The room was totally bare except for a small wooden bench and an oddly-shaped, stone jar. Somewhere in his memory he had seen a jar like that before. But the memory drifted away. On the bench was a neatly folded pile of clothes.

He picked up the clothes. They smelt pretty bad and didn't look too clean. There was a rough tunic, rather like a large T-shirt, and a blanket-shaped piece of thick woollen material which he realised must be a cloak. There was also a leather belt and a pair of rather well worn sandals. When he pulled the tunic on, the rough material scratched his skin, but at least they fitted him. He wondered if he should feel any different. SHARP had told him that the clothes would help him to become the character of Marcus, but he didn't feel anything at all. The tunic came to well below his knees, but he could hitch it up if he pulled the belt tight. The cloak draped over his shoulders fine, and there was a metal pin with which to fasten it. At least he now felt warm. The air inside the room was damp and chilly. Remembering his instructions, he looked in the travel bag and found a small silver disc. He pressed this onto his forehead. It fused into his skin until he could no longer feel it. The thing that SHARP had called a language aid was extremely small. It fitted easily into his ear and after a moment or two, just as with the camera, he couldn't feel it.

With the door open, it took a moment for his eyes to adjust to the brighter sunlight outside, but what he saw stunned him. To either side, an arched colonnade spread out along four outer walls, revealing small doorways at regular intervals. The walls were a dazzling white, but it was what he saw in front of him, in the centre of an enormous courtyard, that made him gasp in amazement. A massive building, shining white, soared skywards, its graceful columns holding up a red tiled roof. Along the edges of the tiles and at the top of the columns were delicate lines of pure gold, dazzling in the sunlight. The building stood on a vast platform, so that it looked as if it were floating in the air. A giant flight of steps led up to what must be the entrance. Brightly coloured lettering stood out on the top of the building, but the words were not in English. Jamie could just make out one word: CLAVDIVS in the inscription. He knew what it was, he had seen this building, in the dark vaulted chamber under Colchester castle, with his classmates gathered round while the guide told them that it had been built for the Emperor Claudius. Claudius was worshipped by the Romans as if he were a god. This was the Temple of Claudius, built in the town of Colchester nearly two thousand years ago!

An uneasy feeling made him look about warily. This beautiful temple with its precinct was supposed to be the hub of Roman Colchester, its very heart. But right now it was completely deserted. He couldn't see a single person, no one climbing up the great steps or strolling in front of the building or the shops around it. No one stood by the giant altar at the entrance. Surely that was where the priests had burnt incense? The place was utterly deserted. There seemed to be a strange foreboding, a tension hanging in the air. Involuntarily, he looked behind him as if expecting someone to be creeping up on him.

There was a flurry of movement on the other side of the precinct. A man was walking along, glancing fearfully from side to side and obviously hoping that he wouldn't be seen. Wrapped in a long white cloak, the man hurried through the colonnade, and then stopped suddenly when he saw Jamie.

'Marcus! Where have you been? I've been searching everywhere for you!' His voice had a hint of authority; he was a man who did not expect to be disobeyed. 'Hurry, we must get home quickly. Cook sent you out hours ago for the fish paste, and she won't be happy being kept waiting this long.'

For a moment Jamie was stunned as he realised he could understand what this Roman man was saying, the language device in his ear must be working. He didn't, of course, quite know what he meant by 'fish paste'. But realisation slowly dawned. In the museum the class had been told how the Romans in Colchester had eaten huge quantities of fish paste. When his class had heard what the ingredients were, they had pulled disgusted faces and then hooted with laughter, at least the boys did. Some of the girls had threatened to be sick on the spot. Fish bones and blood – yuck! That must be what was in the jar in the room, and probably what the disgusting smell was all over his clothes.

'Quick, boy, get the paste,' called the man, and Jamie shot back into the room and picked up the jar. Faugh! At close quarters the smell nearly knocked him over, but he hurried out and followed after the man as he moved quickly along the colonnade to a large gateway.

As they went out of the temple precinct and into the town, they came into what appeared to be an alleyway filled with shops. The street was narrow, with two wheel ruts, one on either side of the cobbled road. The shops had open fronts, with goods of various descriptions hung at the back, or laid out neatly on rough wooden tables. As they hurried along Jamie, despite the weight of the fish paste jar, tried to recognise what each shop was selling. The butcher was easy. There were cuts of meat hanging at the back and birds of different kinds tied together in twos, hanging from the roof. Jamie wasn't sure about the butcher himself. His apron and hands looked filthy and the whole place smelt utterly gross. There was a greengrocer's shop selling fruit and vegetables, although Jamie didn't know what some of the stuff on display actually was. Piles of pots and jars gave away the potter, who was working busily on his wheel at the back. Jamie's mum had taken up pottery for a while but none of her pots could match the ones here. In another shop, a woman was sitting at a loom and piles of brightly coloured cloth were spread across a table. Only a few people were walking along the street, stopping here and there to make some purchases, and when they saw Flavius they bowed low to him. Ah, thought Jamie, the man he was with must be someone important. He wanted to stop and stare, take in the sights, but Flavius was going ahead so fast it was a struggle to keep up.

Just as the jar became almost too heavy to carry, Flavius stopped in front of a door, let into a high wall. It was not an imposing door and had just a simple hook for a latch. Flavius banged on it with his two fists impatiently, and almost at once it opened. An old man, small with hunched shoulders bowed low as Flavius walked in.

'Master, I bid you welcome,' he said, but to Jamie he just gave a wink. To Jamie's relief, he held out his hands for the jar. 'Marcus, cook will whip you when she sees you. She's been waiting for that fish paste and complaining that she can't make preparations for the feast without it. If I were you, I'd make myself scarce for a while to let her calm down.'

'Yes that might be a good idea,' said Flavius. 'Get

back to your room for a while. I'll let you know when I need you. I have something important to do now.'

Flavius walked away to the other side of the courtyard in which they were now standing. Jamie looked around. On three sides, there were graceful columns with a roof above, rather like a verandah, providing shelter from the weather. Jamie could see that there was a fine house beyond the courtyard, and in the centre a fountain bubbled gently into a circular pool surrounded by neatly clipped bushes. The wall with the gate in made up the fourth side of the courtyard, and against that wall were some low, not so spacious buildings.

Probably where the servants live, thought Jamie, as he followed the little old man in that direction. Several people were moving about, some carrying jars and pots, others stoking a small fire to one side of the main building. A few hens were scratching in the dust, and there were several large dogs lolling under the trees. No one took any notice of him as he walked by.

As he had guessed, the servants' quarters were a row of low buildings divided into small rooms, rather like the one in which he had first found himself a short while ago. Not really knowing where he was going, Jamie turned into the second doorway. He found himself in a room with two low beds each covered by a roughly woven blanket. There was a small wooden box in one corner, which was probably for storage or maybe it was a seat. A window above the door let in the light. A boy about his own age was sitting on one of the beds.

As Jamie walked in the boy said, 'Watch yourself, Marcus. Cook's on the warpath. She swore she'd beat you black and blue when she saw you!'

Unsure of quite what to say to this complete stranger, Jamie sat on the other bed and pretended to unfasten his sandal strap, just to give him time to think. None of these people seemed in the least bit surprised to see him, so obviously SHARP's 'cloak of identity' must be working; everyone definitely thought he was Marcus.

'I'd better keep my head down then,' he muttered. Who was this boy? How could he find out his name? But the problem was solved for him as a loud, fierce voice boomed outside in the passageway.

'Bereca, where are you lad? What's the matter with all you lazy young boys today – never around when you're wanted! Come here this minute!'

Bereca (for that was obviously the boy's name) jumped up and made for the door, a cheeky grin on his face.

'Told you, cook's in a really bad mood!' he whispered. 'You'd better not let her know you're in here. She's that mad at you! Remember what happened last time you annoyed her?'

Of course, Jamie didn't have a clue what occasion he was talking about, but he could imagine only too well what might happen if the cook knew where he was. As Bereca left the room, carefully shutting the door behind him, Jamie could hear the cook's angry voice grumbling and threatening all sorts of punishments. The voices faded away and he found himself alone. The shock of what he was doing hit him then, so hard he felt as if he had been winded and he gasped for breath. A million thoughts raced through his mind, uppermost of which was the truly amazing one that he was alive in the Roman town of Colchester, two thousand years before the day he had gone with this class to visit the castle. That castle, old as it was, had not been built at the time he was in now. His hand instinctively went to feel the time/space bag hidden under his tunic and his mobile inside it, his one link with his own time.

The important thing was to fit in as well as he could, pretending to be this boy called Marcus. It was obvious that no one was surprised to see him, so that was a good thing. All he had to do now was try to make sure he always acted as Marcus, do the things that Marcus did and all the while the camera on his forehead would be recording everything. The translation system SHARP had given him worked perfectly. It was so amazing to find himself understanding what people said to him in Latin and talking in Latin, even though he was clearly thinking in English. That alone was proof of SHARP's amazingly advanced science, if he needed further proof. What he couldn't understand was that although SHARP had given him lots of information, not much of it was about what he was to do once he arrived in Roman Colchester. He knew he had to listen to everyone as much as he could and watch, very carefully, everyone and everything around him – and by doing just that he had managed so far.

He began to feel incredibly tired and sleepy. He felt as if he had been awake for days. He struggled to keep his eyes open but it was no good. He lay down on the small bed, pulled the blanket over himself and fell fast asleep. The next thing he knew Bereca was shaking him awake.

CHAPTER 7

A Roman Servant

'Come on, Marcus, the Master needs you.' Bereca walked over to the other bed and sat down still looking at Jamie, who hadn't said a word yet. 'You are to serve at the feast tonight. You know that don't you? I know you have not been long with our Master Flavius, but you come from a good Roman family, you will be fine.'

Jamie stared at Bereca.

'You look as if you have seen ghost, Marcus. What's the matter with you, aren't you well?'

'I don't know, I feel a bit bad.'

'You and everyone else. Don't tell me you've been getting premonitions as well.'

'No, of course not.'

'I'll get you some water. Just get up and make yourself presentable.' Bereca quickly left the room

Jamie stood up, straightened his rumpled tunic and fastened his sandals. Bereca came back in with a cup of water and handed it to him. Jamie realised that he was incredibly thirsty. He drank the water down in one go.

'Bereca, thanks. You're a mate. I feel much better.'

'Good. And by the way, I think cook's got over her bad temper now that she's got the meal in hand. She's let you off on account of you being new to your position.'

'That's a relief to know.'

Together they made their way out and over to the fine house. Dusk had fallen, and soft lights filled the courtyard and sent shadows flickering here and there. The house seemed much busier than it had been earlier, and as they entered, Marcus could see a number of men standing around, talking quietly in groups. From their clothes he could see that they were wealthy, and Bereca bowed low to each of them. Jamie did the same, and then he saw Flavius standing by a couch next to a fine, but very low, marble table.

'Wine boy, give our guests wine!'

For a moment Jamie panicked, but Bereca had already picked up a large stone jar and was moving amongst the guests, pouring wine into their goblets, so he did the same. He noticed that the men hardly looked at him as he did so; a servant obviously did not count for much in Roman Colchester.

After a while, the guests moved to the low

couches and lounged down on them. Servants appeared with the meal, trays of meat, carefully sliced, what looked like figs and olives, loaves of bread and various kinds of other fruits. Jamie could see small pots containing sauces, but none of them smelt like the fish paste he had carried back to the house. Cook might be a tetchy old woman, but she knew how to prepare a good feast; she must know how to make that dreadful fish paste taste good. Jamie moved to stand beside Flavius, as it was becoming obvious that he was the man's personal servant and was there to attend to his every wish.

The men started tucking into the food. How peculiar, Jamie thought, to eat lying down, rather than sitting at a table. Surely, they would get stomach ache eating like that? The way they ate was a bit disgusting, using their hands to put food in their mouths and throwing their heads back to drop in a particularly tasty morsel. They obviously thought nothing of talking with their mouths full. Jamie was fascinated and then had to stifle a laugh as one man let out an enormous rumbling burp and, as if in answer, another man did the same. They all ate enormous helpings and the wine flowed freely, and no one seemed the worse for it.

As they ate, Jamie could hear snatches of the conversations. They talked about their families, the town and its business and the crops out on the farms. There was much interest in the price of cattle, which amused Jamie remembering his talk in the office with his dad going on about farm prices; some things it seemed didn't change, even over two thousand years. But when the meal finished the jovial talk stopped and Flavius signalled to Jamie and Bereca to leave the room. As soon as they were outside Bereca said:

'You know, something's wrong.'

'Wrong? What do you mean?'

'The master never holds a feast for so many of the town's elders all at once. And surely you've realised that it didn't last long? Normally they'd be eating until well into the early hours. I have never known him tell us servants to leave? Someone should be there to pour the wine.'

Jamie remembered his arrival in the temple precinct and how it had seemed strange that it had been so deserted. Was there something wrong, and was this why SHARP had sent him?

Bereca led the way into the courtyard and the boys climbed a flight of steps leading to the top of the wall around the house. From there they could see out across the town. A few lights flickered here and there and then beyond that – utter blackness. Jamie, used to lights everywhere late at night, found the darkness unnerving. What was out there beyond the lights of the town? A shiver ran down his spine and he pulled the thick cloak tightly around him, ignoring its smell.

'So, why do you think the master has called all these men here tonight?' Jamie asked.

Bereca turned towards him. Jamie found it hard to see the expression on his face in the darkness, but could tell from how he leaned in towards him and lowered his voice that he didn't want anyone else to hear what he was going to say.

'This morning, in the market place I heard some men talking. They said there's trouble brewing. The tribes are arming themselves.'

Suddenly Jamie felt the hair standing up on his neck. In the excitement of travelling back in time, he hadn't thought too much about the date. It had been exciting enough to hear that he was going back to Roman times, but the date... AD 60? He repeated the date in his head, it was an easy one to remember, and then it came to him; the guide at the castle had said that AD 60 was the date of the revolt by the Iceni tribe. They had risen up against the Romans and destroyed the town. The Iceni, led by their mighty queen, Boudica, had destroyed the town.

Carefully, so as to avoid saying anything to upset his new friend, he asked Bereca, 'Is it true then? Are they coming here? Now?'

'I think the elders are here to discuss how to defend the city. I know some of the townspeople have left already. I don't think we have enough soldiers to defend the town, and there's no wall to keep the tribes out. I think they have already sent to Londinium for reinforcements.'

Londinium – that was London. Fifty miles away at least, less than an hour by train, but in this age when everything moved on horseback or by foot, it would, Jamie calculated, take at least a couple of days.

'Maybe they won't get here in time?'

'Exactly,' said Bereca. 'And that's why they're all here. They should have seen the warning signs before, but they didn't. Even if they have sent to Londinium for reinforcements, it is not a sure thing that Londinium will respond quickly. There's only a handful of soldiers in this town. We won't stand a chance.'

There was movement in the courtyard below them. A small group of mounted soldiers, dressed exactly as Jamie had seen on the models in the museum, came through the gates. They jumped from their horses, handing the reins to servants and went into the house. Jamie could hear urgent voices for a moment or two, then the soldiers reappeared. They went out into the street and Jamie heard the clatter of horses' hooves as they rode away into the distance. At the same time the guests left the house hurriedly, and silence fell.

Bereca turned towards Jamie and this time he could see his wide eyes shining in the dark.

'It's started,' he breathed. 'At last something's going to happen.'

As he lay on his narrow bed later that night, listening to Bereca's soft breathing on the other side of the room, Jamie wondered what the new day would bring. He tried to remember what Mrs. Taylor had said about Boudica. They had seen a film presentation of the Iceni revolt, and in his mind he heard, over and over again, the roaring of flames and the screaming voices as the Temple of Claudius burnt to the ground. Roman Colchester had been utterly destroyed, that much he remembered, but why? Why did this happen? Why had the mighty Romans been defeated by the very people they had beaten in battle only a few years earlier? If reinforcements from Londinium had been sent for, why had they not arrived in time to save the town? Why was the town not defended? And, as Bereca had pointed out, why was there no wall? There had been a wall around Colchester at some time. He'd often seen bits of it, but maybe that had been built later in Norman times when the castle had been built? Slowly, Jamie drifted off to sleep. Only a few hours latter someone was banging loudly on the door.

It was very early, before the cocks had crowed and the first rays of a cold winter sun broke over the horizon. Jamie and Bereca joined all of the servants gathered in the kitchen where a fire had already been started. Something unusual was happening; a tall, burly man (obviously the one in charge of the household) called them to order and told them to listen carefully.

'The master demands our presence. He has something to tell us.' The man's eyes flickered here and there over the little group. 'Be quick, all of you, follow me. We must not keep him waiting.'

Silently, they crossed the courtyard and entered the house. Flavius came out from one of the rooms to meet them, and overnight he seemed to have aged. His face was lined and grey. A tall, graceful woman stood beside him, and Jamie guessed that she must be his wife, as the others bowed low before her. She never once took her eyes from her husband's face as he spoke quickly and quietly to the small group of servants, all of whom were pulling their cloaks tightly around them. Jamie noticed, with surprise, that he was doing the same, and that he found it hard to keep his hands steady as he did so.

'You will have heard the rumours spreading around the town. I cannot lie to you. We are all in great danger. The tribes have raised an army against us and are marching on the town. They have sworn they will destroy it.'

There was silence, broken only by one old woman beginning to sob. No one took any notice of her, everyone's eyes were fixed on Flavius. It was as if they were all waiting to be told what to do, unable to make up their own minds. Perhaps they were numbed with shock, too frightened to do or say anything. But as Jamie glanced at the people around him, he saw something else in their faces apart from blind panic; it was trust. Flavius was their master, he would look after them; he would know what to do.

'We must hurry.' Flavius spoke urgently. 'The city elders held a meeting here last night and made a decision. Those who can, if it is still possible, must leave the town with all haste. Do not try to take too much with you. There is no time and you must travel quickly. Get down to the harbour. Hopefully you will find a boat to get you out of here. We do not yet know exactly where the Iceni are, but it would not be safe to use the roads out of the town. If there are no boats and your escape route is blocked, the only safe place in the town is the Temple. Last night we devised a plan of how best to deploy the few soldiers we have here. They will focus on defending the Temple. The spirit of our divine emperor will guard those who take refuge in there and it is a strong building. But, although I am your master, each one of you must decide what you want to do. I will not order you. Hurry, for there is so little time. I will be going with my dear wife...' he turned and looked at the woman beside him, 'my dear wife, Julia Flavia, to the Temple.'

All at once, everyone began to speak, voices high pitched with fear. They clung on to each other, their eyes pleading.

'What shall we do?' the cry was the same from everyone. The fear was contagious, and Jamie fought down a rising tide of panic. He put his hand to his side and felt the travel bag, stuck there firmly. He had to control an urge to take out the phone and press the red phoenix bird app there and then, but part of his mind said: no, not yet, not yet, wait...

He heard Flavius's voice again.

'Although the situation is grave, all hope is not yet lost. The town elders have already sent an urgent message to Londinium to the Procurator. No doubt he will have already sent troops to help us, and they will destroy the rebel queen's army. Barbarians are no match for the might of Rome.'

All around him the others nodded and Jamie could feel their sense of relief at this news, but looking at Flavius he somehow knew that this was a false hope and that their master did not truly believe what he had just said. The look on Bereca's face told him the same.

'We must do what we can to ensure our own safety,' Flavius went on. 'It is hard to know who will get here first, the relief force from Londinium or the Iceni. So now each one of you must decide whether to try and escape or come with me to the Temple. At least we can defend ourselves there until help arrives. Gather only what you can carry, but decide quickly, before it is too late.'

Flavius turned to his wife and, holding her hand tightly, went to leave the room. Almost as an afterthought he motioned to the two boys to approach him.

'Marcus, you have not been with me long, but you have served me well. What will you do? Will you follow your Master or try to escape?'

Jamie's mind raced, fear and panic chasing round in his head. It was as if he was Marcus, not a boy from the twenty-first century who had an amazing scientific means of escape. It was as if he was facing the same fate as everyone else! He desperately wanted to run, to dash out of this doomed Roman villa and get out into the countryside and hide from whatever was in store for them all. But he steadied himself and looked into the face of the Roman.

'Master, I... I'll come with you.' he stammered.

Flavius smiled down at him and put a hand on his shoulder. 'Good boy, I'm glad. And you, Bereca, what will you do? You have been a faithful servant for a long time.' For a moment, the other boy looked undecided, and then a smile broke out on his face.

'I too will come with you, Master, I will serve you and your wife always.'

'You are both true and loyal servants. When we return to Rome, you will not be sorry you have made this choice, for we will return to Rome, of that I am sure. Now quickly, fetch all you need and come with me.'

Jamie and Bereca followed the others back to the servants' quarters. Bereca picked up the blanket on his bed, folded and put it over his arm. He took a simple iron bracelet out of the wooden box and put it in a small bag that he hung across his shoulders.

'Marcus, aren't you going to take your treasures?' he asked, passing a small bag, similar to his own, to Jamie.

'Of course,' Jamie said putting the thong of the bag over his head as Bereca had done, having no idea what it contained. They then headed back to the main house as Flavius had instructed them. Jamie had not been to this part of the house before, but he realised that it was much finer than the other rooms he had seen. The walls were painted and the floor was covered in a beautiful mosaic, which Jamie was sure he had seen before. Four fish-like animals were arranged around the sides and in the middle were two winged children fighting with their fists. There was hardly time to take it all in before Flavius and his wife appeared from a doorway in the far side and they set off together.

CHAPTER 8

A Temple Falls

It was very early morning and the sky was dark, threatening rain or sleet. Jamie was aware of other people moving stealthily in the same direction towards the temple of Claudius. Some were carrying bundles and all were muffled in their cloaks as if trying to keep out the fear, which threatened to erupt into blind panic. They passed one weeping woman who tightly clasped a new-born baby to her, and a very old man who could only hobble slowly, being encouraged along by a young boy. As they came nearer to the precinct the crowds increased, until when they stood in front of the great Temple itself, there must have been several hundred people.

A man was standing at the top of the steps, surrounded by a few soldiers. By now it was getting lighter, and red torches threw out a dim light that cast huge shadows on the walls of the Temple. Flavius told Jamie and Bereca to wait with his wife and hurriedly mounted the steps to talk to the man with the soldiers. It was obvious that this man was someone of importance. Just after Falvius had joined him, he held up his hand and spoke to the crowd who fell silent. Flavius standing next to him, occasionally whispered something into his ear.

'People of Colchester,' the man called out, 'I cannot lie to you, and some of you already know what I am about to say. The Iceni and their queen are less than a day's march from our town, and moving quickly. They are destroying everything in their path.' There were some muffled cries from the crowd as they heard this, and one woman began to scream until a man standing next to her put his hand over her mouth to silence her.

'We will take refuge in the Temple. No rebel army can destroy such a mighty building, and our emperor, the divine Claudius, will look kindly on us and the gods will give us their protection. Be patient, the troops I have sent for from Londinium will get here in time to save us. Do not fear...'

But at the back of the crowd a woman began to wail, her voice sounding frighteningly eerie in the half-light. Jamie turned and saw her wild eyes and straggly hair and noticed how those around her began to move away, leaving her to stand like an island in a stormy sea, her arms waving wildly in the air.

'It's no good,' she screamed. 'Did I not hear with my own ears how the statues near the Temple began to cry out with a mighty wailing? It is an omen – the gods have spoken. We cannot be saved!'

Others too began to call out, telling of strange and unnatural portents that they had also seen in the last few days. The crowd shifted uneasily, and the man on the steps realised that if he did not do something now, the panic would begin to spread and there would be a riot. His voice cut through the wailing.

'Enough! Why listen to this idle old crone? Colchester is a mighty town, and the Roman Empire is greater still. This is the capital of the province of Britannia and it will never fall to a rabble army – never!'

All this time Jamie had kept his eyes on the man who was speaking, but something – he never found out what – suddenly made him turn round. The crowd were standing at the foot of the steps leading up to the Temple, craning forward to listen to the city elder. Behind them, perched on a slender stone column, was the statue of a woman. In her outstretched hand she held a crown of leaves, and huge wings spread out behind her as if she were flying. Like an angel, Jamie thought. She perched gracefully on her column, but as he watched the statue began to move from side to side, slowly at first and then faster and faster. Others in the crowd turned to look, and Jamie heard a noise like a huge intake of breath as the people realised what was happening. As if in slow motion, the statue began to topple and then crashed to the ground, smashing into pieces on the floor at their feet. For a moment there was a stunned silence, and then the screaming began. Wails of terrible fear filled the air, but above it all Jamie heard the voice of the old woman:

'See! See where she lies! The Winged Victory has fallen, and fallen with her back towards the city gates! She is fleeing, fleeing from the enemy!'

At that there was pandemonium. Jamie felt himself being pushed this way and that as the crowd ran wildly in terror, hardly knowing where they were going. He lost sight of Bereca and Flavius's wife. People tore at each other in their fear, hands clutching wildly at anything they could reach. Somehow he managed to push himself behind the base of the altar and crouched there in fear as the crowd seethed around him. Suddenly Bereca, holding the arm of Flavius's wife, unceremoniously pushed her into the small space and climbed in after her breathing hard, his hair dishevelled. They were squashed together tightly. Jamie could feel Julia's breath on his cheek.

There was a sweet smell of flowers, reminding Jamie of the very few occasions when his mother wore perfume; it was unbelievably strange being so close to this elegant Roman woman.

'Be quiet and don't move – the soldiers will sort this out!' Bereca hissed at him, just audible through the noise around them.

For a few wild moments there was total bedlam. Crouched beside Julia Flavia, Jamie hardly dared to open his eyes whilst the noise of the crowd roared above his head. It was impossible to make out what was happening, but then he could pick out a different sound – the clash of steel on steel. The soldiers had waded into the crowd and were striking out left and right at whoever was in their path. Slowly, slowly (but to Jamie, squeezed down by the altar it seemed to go on for ever) the soldiers gained control and the crowd began to calm down. By the time the three of them emerged from their hiding place, the people were quiet and the city elder had begun to speak again.

For a few moments it was hard to tell whether the people's fear would prevail or whether they would listen to the man's voice of reason. Jamie could feel the crowd's emotions being tossed this way and that like a tiny boat in a stormy sea, but gradually they fell silent, even though eyes darted fearfully as if expecting to see the Iceni and their queen rising out of the ground under their very feet. Again the man's voice rang out.

'Come, we do not fear a noisy rabble and their ragged queen. Will you let your own fear defeat you? Let us move now, good people. Go into the Temple with your families, and when the great doors are shut we will be safe. Londinium will not fail us – help will arrive in time.'

At this point, Jamie wanted to scream at him, tell him he was completely wrong.

We'll die like rats in a trap, he thought, but as the crowd of people nodded their assent he was slowly pushed forward, up the steps towards the Temple. Anxious not to be separated from Julia and Bereca again, he made his way up the steps with them. Only now, he was hugging tightly onto the travel bag, his only means of escape. Yes, it was still there, now almost part of his actual body. At the top of the steps Flavius pulled his wife to one side and Jamie and Bereca went in on their own.

Once through the double row of columns at the front of the Temple, Jamie could see that the inner shrine was large. It was hard to see exactly how big as there were no windows at all. All the light was coming through the open doors. If these were shut, it would be pitch black inside. The atmosphere was stuffy, with the cloying smell of old incense hanging around them. More and more people pushed in, but gradually people began to settle and try to find a space on the floor to rest. An uneasy silence fell, broken only by the sound of breathing and the occasional whimpering of a frightened child. Jamie felt sure that everyone could hear the loud, fearful thumping of his heart, but perhaps they were too busy listening to their own. Torches were lit to give more light, but the smoke, the sickly smell of the burning pitch and the many unwashed bodies, made the air heavy.

Hours seemed to pass. The door of the shrine remained open, with the few armed soldiers left in the town guarding the entrance, their spears and swords glinting in the half light of the dark winter's day. Occasionally Jamie heard whispers of what sounded like prayers, and once in the distance a horse's galloping feet. Now that people were settled in the Temple with their things, some would go outside and walk about before coming in to claim their patch of temple floor. It was almost like when twenty-first century crowds turned up early for some event, such as the first day of the sales or a royal wedding or jubilee, and spent days and nights carefully guarding their hard-won space. Jamie stood up and took a few steps towards the door trying not to tread on any of the people who were sitting or lying around him. Bereca stood up beside him, his face ghostly pale in the dim interior light. Together they moved forward, looking for Flavius and his wife Julia. Eventually they found them sitting near the open door, and the man who had spoken to the crowd a few hours before was with them. As the two boys approached, Julia whispered something to Flavius who looked very serious and then nodded. When they got close, Flavius stretched out his hand and placed it first on Bereca's shoulder and then on Jamie's.

'Thank you, both of you. You have done me a great service today.'

'It is mainly Bereca you need to thank,' said Jamie simply and Flavius nodded, recognising the boy's honesty.

Then Flavius spoke gently to his wife.

'My dear, wait here. Aquilius and I must go to speak to the soldiers. We will take the boys with us.' His wife raised her hand to clutch at his cloak as if begging him to stay, but he shook his head.

'Courage, my love. You must set an example to the people. We will not be long, and your servants will remain with you.' He nodded to a young girl standing next to Julia, and an old man who Jamie recognised as the servant who had opened the door for them when he was carrying the fish paste jar. They both responded with a bow.

Bereca and Jamie followed the two men out into the precinct. Apart from the handful of soldiers guarding the door, the precinct was totally deserted.

'Your master tells me that you are loyal and faithful servants. Does that mean that we can trust you with our lives?' Aquilius spoke quietly but urgently to the two boys. 'Are you brave enough to put yourselves in great danger for the sake of this city?'

'My lord knows I am not a coward. I will serve Rome to the end,' said Bereca.

Flavius smiled briefly, but when he spoke his voice was deadly serious.

'I know. You have shown me that already today. That is why I have chosen you and Marcus. I could have asked twenty others at least, but I chose you two because I know that I can put my life and that of my family in your hands and you will guard it safely. We need you to do something that will take a great deal of courage.'

Jamie felt a new surge of fear and excitement run through his body; it was as if the floodgates were opened and he was being swept along with little choice. He bowed low before the two men and the words that came out of his mouth were like nothing he had ever spoken before: 'My lords, tell us what you want us to do.'

When darkness came an hour or so later, Jamie and Bereca found themselves stealing quietly away from the Temple. They had no burning torch to help them because they could not risk being seen, but the light from the moon was just enough to guide them through the deserted streets of the town and on towards the south gate. Against his chest Jamie wore a soft bag containing Aquilius's great ring, as proof that they were the messengers of the town elders. The boys ran silently, looking this way and that, until they reached the outer limits of the town. They were following the instructions they had been given by Aquilius and Flavius who had explained that the one chance for the town was the element of surprise. The soldiers from Londonium needed to be shown the way to the Temple as quickly and as quietly as possible. There the soldiers could conceal themselves in the surrounding streets, and ambush the Iceni as they entered the precinct. But the Romans would be outnumbered so the element of surprise was vitally important.

'Don't forget,' Flavius had said to them. 'Boudica has met little opposition so far and she thinks that the town is full of women, children and old men, with only a handful of soldiers to protect them. We want her to believe that, so that she will think that we are easy pickings and that will make her careless. She must not know about the reinforcements. This is a dangerous mission we give you. The main army of the Iceni is somewhere to the north of the town, but they may well have sent scouts to surround us. We do not need to tell you what will happen if they find you before the troops arrive.'

The boys were now crouching down low behind the south gate, their ears straining into the darkness beyond. Before them, silvery in the moonlight, was the road to Londinium. The eerie shapes of tombstones lined the road on each side like pale ghosts. The soldiers would come along the road, and they must be warned. Although Boudica and her army would be coming from the north, on the other side of the town, scouts were certain to be sent to check all roads. It seemed as if they sat for hours, straining their eyes out into the darkness for any sign of the reinforcements. The cold ate into their bones and a white frost covered the ground, but all they could do was pull their cloaks tighter around them and try to stop their teeth from chattering too loudly. Sometimes they whispered to each other, more in an effort to keep their spirits up than for any other reason. But Jamie was burning to ask Bereca a question; he knew how dangerous things were, but he needed to know why. Why had the Iceni risen up against the Romans? Quietly he whispered to the boy beside him.

'Bereca, why is this happening? If I am to die, I need to know why.'

Bereca turned towards him and Jamie heard the hopelessness in his voice as he answered the question.

'Marcus,' he said. 'Everyone knows why – everyone that is, but the Romans themselves. You cannot take away a man's land and expect him to like you for it. You can't just confiscate all his property and hand it over to one of your own retired soldiers. You know how angry people are, Marcus, and that anger has been boiling up for a long time.'

There was a long silence and Jamie thought that Bereca had finished, but he started speaking again, slowly, as if he was not really sure of what he was saying, his voice filled with uncertainty.

'You know I'm an Iceni by birth but I owe my life and the lives of my family to Flavius, and I will serve him to the end. But his people were wrong to treat us with such disdain, to take away our land and put their own men in our place. They conquered us and then they rubbed our noses in the dirt.'

Jamie was startled by the anger in Bereca's voice, and surprised too that he was not actually a Roman.

'I suppose I've never thought about it,' he said.

'No, Marcus, you wouldn't have thought of it. Your family came from Rome and you are a Roman. You have never learnt, like I have, to work as hard as you can to get what you want.'

Bereca's words startled Jamie; they were an echo of words he heard many times before: … 'work as hard as you can to get what you want'.

'My tribe is full of proud warriors, Marcus.' Bereca went on. ' No men are braver. But we couldn't stand up to the might of Rome. There were so many soldiers and they just overwhelmed us. But it wasn't enough to conquer us – they had to shame us as well.'

A noise out in the dark in front of the gate brought both boys to full alert. Hardly daring to breathe they waited to see if it would come again, but the silence of the night remained unbroken; probably some animal on its nocturnal wanderings.

'Boudica and her tribe are proud people. They thought that if they gave in to the Romans' demands they'd be left alone, but oh no. Conquer them, shame and humiliate them, then tax them! The Romans lent them money and then demanded it back again when they knew the tribesmen couldn't repay it. But to shame the queen herself and her family!' Bereca shuddered and did not go on.

'Do you hate the Romans? Do you want the Iceni to destroy the town?'

Again there was a long pause.

'Even if the Iceni win here in Colchester, they will not destroy the Romans,' Bereca answered. 'I can't remember living in an Iceni village, but I do know that the Iceni do not have houses like the Romans or live like the Romans. My mother and father died when I was very young and Flavius took me in and his servants looked after me. My two sisters and oldest brother were taken as slaves to Rome, but Flavius tells me they have been well treated and that my brother has won his freedom and is now a Roman. I too could be a Roman one day. Can you imagine what it would be like to live in Rome? Now that is probably not going to happen.' Bereca's voice sounded tired, flat and empty. 'If the Iceni attack, I will stand by Flavius and defend him with my life. Besides, they are hardly likely to ask us if we support them as they raise their spears against us. Flavius has been a good master to me, and my family. I owe him much.'

Jamie didn't speak. It was hard to know what to say. He had known Bereca for such a short time, but he desperately wanted to help him. Could he warn him of what was about to happen? Bereca could disappear into the night and get to Londinium, perhaps then he could eventually get to Rome, as he dreamed?

'Bereca, I...' he began, but suddenly Bereca pulled him down, hissing quietly, 'Don't move, someone's coming.'

The two of them crouched down, hardly daring to breathe. They stared out across the silent countryside. It was pitch black now; the moon was hidden behind clouds. Then, there it was: a faint glint of steel and the sound of feet moving rhythmically towards them. The soldiers from Londinium had arrived! The two slowly stood up to meet the marching troop, relieved that at last they could dare to believe the town might be saved.

But as the men drew near, Jamie was shocked.

This was not what they had been hoping for. These men were exhausted. Covered in mud from the road, they were poorly armed, and why were there so few of them? Flavius had asked the Procurator to send an army to defend the town, but there could not have been more than two hundred men altogether, and their commander seemed ill at ease, almost ashamed of his little troop. When they came near, the two boys held up their hands in a gesture to stop the soldiers and Jamie stepped forward to show the commander Aquilius's ring.

'Sir, you do not know how glad we are to see you. My master and the town elders have sent us to bring you as quickly as possible to the Temple. Boudica and her army are very close. Please follow us quickly.'

Jamie hoped that the disappointment did not sound too obvious in his voice, but he could see it plainly in Bereca's eyes. Bereca knew, these men would never be able to make stand against the Iceni hordes. Why had Londinium failed them? They stood no chance, no chance at all!

Suddenly a thought came to Jamie and he knew what he must do. He took off the bag around his neck that had held the ring, slipped the ring into the bag and said to Bereca, 'I was told by Flavius to tell you that as soon as the soldiers arrived I was to guide them to the precinct. You must set out and walk to Londinium. You must take this ring with you to show to the Procurator and tell him that you have been chosen to bring him news of Colchester's stand against the Iceni.' Jamie held out the bag with the ring in it towards his friend.

'But...but I don't understand,' said Bereca, taking the bag, but looking stunned.

'You don't have to,' said Jamie convinced now that he was doing the right thing. 'You must just do as your master, Flavius, bids, and Bereca, please will you look after my treasurers in this bag.' Jamie pulled the small bag he had been given earlier that day and held it out to Bereca. 'Goodbye, friend. I will see you in Rome, one day. Go now!' Jamie stretched out his hand towards Bereca, who still looked uncertain.

'Go now, I have the authority of Flavius,' Jamie said again, with conviction. He knew his lies might just be saving his new friend's life. The two clasped their hands for a moment and then Bereca turned and started walking up the road towards Londinium. After a few paces, he broke into a run. Jamie watched for a moment and then signalled to the commander of the troop to follow him.

Somehow, he remembered the exact route he had taken earlier with Bereca and led the sorry band of men into the precinct. Aquilius and Flavius came down the Temple steps to meet the commander. They made no attempt at concealing their anger and disappointment. Why had Londinium sent so few men? The commander had no answer for them. With as much enthusiasm as they could muster Flavius and Aquilius started outlining their plan for the defence of the Temple. But, even as they did so, the wild, harsh sound of a Celtic battle horn made everyone freeze. The sound was coming from the direction of the north gate. She was here: Boudica and her army had reached the outskirts of the town! They must have crossed the river and were climbing the hill on which the Temple stood. They would be in the precinct in minutes.

The massive doors of the shrine clanged shut. People pressed close together for comfort. Some were whimpering or crying. The voice of an officer rang out over the hubbub, trying to gain control, to stop fear turning into outright panic. By now Flavius had rejoined his wife, who sat weeping silently. Flavius put his arm around her and then saw Jamie, crouching silently beside her. He did not mention that Bereca was not with him, but Jamie wanted to tell him what he had done.

'I told Bereca to go to the Procurator in Londinium,' he whispered. 'I gave him the ring.'

Flavius looked at him intensely for a moment and then simply said, 'You did well, Marcus.' Then in a louder voice he continued. 'Do not be afraid. We can hold out in the Temple for days, and the Iceni will never break in. Another relief force will come – you can be sure of that.' Jamie realised that his master had pitched his voice loud enough for those around him to hear, but both of them knew that rescue would never come and that the end was near.

The noise outside the Temple walls was becoming louder and louder. There were more and more blasts from the strident Celtic horn and a tumult of shouts, cries and the clash of steel. The tired Roman soldiers were putting up a fight. Jamie was glad he could not see the carnage going on outside the Temple walls. After a while, the smell of burning filled the air, and the fierce crackling of flames and the roar of fires could be heard above the din. Colchester was burning. The noise got louder and louder. Still some inside the Temple clung on to the hope that they would be safe, as if the Iceni would not know they were there, hidden inside. But where else would they be? Jamie could picture in his mind the queen of the Iceni, standing tall and proud in her war chariot, her mouth curling into a savage smile as she looked at the hated Temple of Claudius standing in the burning ruins of the once mighty town, the Roman capital of Britainnia.

The vibrating of his phone against his side made him jump. He reached for it, feeling the press of people all around him. It hardly mattered if anyone saw what he was doing, but even so, he pulled his cloak far forward over his head as if he were trying to shut out the terrible din outside the Temple. He carefully flicked on the screen and read the message.

Jamie, we are aware that you are in extreme danger, but our transporter is experiencing difficulties at present. Power is right down. There is just enough to bring you back, but you will only have one chance . We will leave it to your judgement to decide the best moment to return but immediately after you press the red phoenix key in the code as quickly as possible. Any delay, even of a few seconds, could be extremely dangerous. Good luck.

As the message slowly faded from the screen,

Jamie could feel his heart beating so wildly against his ribs that he felt as if he would throw up. Soon the Iceni would be battering down the doors to the shrine, and he could not bear to think what would then happen to the people inside, and to him too if he couldn't get away. Should he try to go now? No, his hands were shaking so badly and he had to be absolutely sure he would get it right. There wouldn't be another chance. Wait a bit, just a bit longer.

The noise of thudding filled the air as some giant object slammed against the doors of the shrine. The people shrank back in fear, but they had nowhere to go. The soldiers at the door moved forward, swords raised, ready for action, but futile against the size of the mob outside. Thud… thud… thud. How long did it go on for? The doors shook, the timbers creaked and groaned, but they did not give way. The doors held, and the screaming mob outside could not get in. For a brief moment in time relief spread through the people of Colchester. Had they escaped the wrath of Boudica and her tribe?

By now the air inside the Temple was foul and hardly breathable; some of the old and weak were close to death and the water had run out. The screaming din of the attackers outside never ceased, as if they sensed that victory would soon be theirs. Suddenly it became quiet, but then they could hear sounds of drunken revelry and fighting. It seemed as if the tribesmen had looted the town's wine cellars and drunk more than they could hold. Perhaps now they were sleeping it off. No one knew what would happen next.

Then there was a strange noise high above them on the Temple roof, a scratching sound as if some giant bird was hopping around on the tiles. More scratches followed, then banging and thudding.

'Look!' shouted Flavius 'They're on the roof!' But what could the people do? They had no weapons, and the roof was too high to reach. All eyes turned upwards as the tiles began to lift and wild savage faces peered down. The light from torches filled the Temple with a fierce glow and then ropes snaked down through the holes. Jamie felt a firm hand on his shoulder and looked up into the face of Flavius. He couldn't read the expression in the man's eyes, but somehow it seemed as if he knew – knew about everything. Jamie would never forget his voice and what he said, 'Now Marcus, now is the time. Don't argue – you cannot change what will happen. Do it... Do it now!'

Jamie threw off the cloak, undid the sandals and ripped of the tunic. For one last time he looked at Flavius; dust and stones poured down from the large hole in the roof above, covering him like a shroud. His hand felt the phone firm under his fingers. Without a moment's hesitation he pressed the red phoenix and then the numbers 16008. The chaos in the Temple seemed for a moment to spin round him, but through the other noises, a high-pitched whine enveloped him. Then... Nothing.

CHAPTER 9

Time Travel Pain

Jamie found himself sitting on a bench in the first aid room at Colchester Castle, his mobile in his hand. He was shaking from head to foot and nearly dropped his mobile. He dashed into the staff toilet where he had left his clothes and quickly got dressed.

Mrs. Taylor was worried about him. First that strange behaviour in the vaults, and then how dreadful he had looked when he came back from the first aid room – as if he'd seen a ghost. He'd hardly said a word all the way home, just that he had a really bad headache and wanted to be left alone. He even refused a bar of chocolate that Max had saved for him from his lunch box. He was deathly pale and his eyes looked somehow haunted.

'I don't know what's wrong with him,' Mrs. Taylor said to the headteacher when they got back to school. 'He looks as if he's been in the wars.' The headteacher phoned Mrs. Tate who came straight away to pick him up an hour before the end of school.

'Come on, Jamie, let's get home,' said his mum. 'Bed for you, and in the morning I'll take you to the doctor if you're no better.'

Jamie didn't mind sliding under his duvet and being left alone in his room. It would give him a chance to get in touch with SHARP. Leika was the only person he could talk to about what had happened. He'd never be able to tell anyone else, they'd think he was mad, or a liar.

After dialling 16008, he didn't have long to wait. In no time at all his phone vibrated and a message flashed up on the screen. It was Leika.

Hello Jamie. That was close — we nearly lost you. We've had real trouble at this end — the transporter began to malfunction at just the wrong moment and we underestimated how long it would take to fix it.

There was a pause, and then more words flashed up.

Jamie, are you alright?

Alright? How could Jamie answer that after what he'd seen? He didn't reply. The message went on.

OK Jamie. SHARP is aware of the dangerous situation you were in. Time travel isn't always pleasant, but we badly needed to update our records about Roman Colchester, and you certainly did that for us. We know that our operations can cause some stress to our time travellers. But we were very impressed at how you dealt with your trip and we'll be in touch with you again shortly. You may not appreciate it right now, but you will always remember, and treasure, the experiences you had in Roman times. Now go to sleep, go to sleep...sleep.

As Jamie read these words the screen began to glow in soothing green colours, and he felt his eyes close and his head fall back on the pillows. When his mum came back to see him later that evening he was fast asleep, still holding his mobile in his limp fingers. Carefully, Mrs. Tate took it from him and put it on his bedside table.

The next morning, Jamie seemed to be back to his old self. At first, when his mum came into his room to tell him to get up, he moaned, as usual, about having to go to school, almost as if it was a habit. Then, suddenly he was out of bed and getting ready with an eagerness that was very different to how he usually felt. In the back of his mind, Bereca's words echoed: 'As a Roman, you have never learnt to work as hard as I have.' He went downstairs feeling incredibly hungry and ate a huge breakfast.

'Anyone would think you hadn't eaten properly for days,' his mum smiled at him. At school he got ribbed for nearly fainting in the vaults, but Jamie could handle that. The thing that surprised Mrs. Taylor was how confidently he answered all the questions about the school trip and Roman Colchester.

'Anyone would think that you'd actually been there,' said Adam Pitt at lunch time.

'Well,' said Jamie, 'perhaps I was there,' and his friends all smirked at Adam's surprised face.

'You'd believe anything, wouldn't you?' they sniggered. As for Max, he was just glad that Jamie was back to his usual self again.

In the staff room that evening, Mrs. Taylor read through the written work the class had done on the trip. When she came to Jamie's, she couldn't quite believe what she was reading.

'Look at this,' she said to some of the other teachers in there. 'This is Jamie Tate's account of the Boudican revolt. It's good, really good. There is so much detail in here. He's written that they attacked from the north, and I can't remember giving them that information. He must have been doing research before the visit. I have never had a piece of work like this from him before.'

When one of the other teachers read it, an amazed expression spread across her face. 'That trip really captured his imagination, alright. Reading that you'd think he'd actually been there.'

Over the next few weeks, although Jamie knew Leika was right: he would never forget Roman Colchester, the rawer details seemed to blur and fade, so that his memories were not as painful. He could remember vividly what had happened and the people he had met, but not the huge fear and full horror as the Iceni faces peered down through the roof, or the raging sound of battle outside the Temple walls. It was several days before he could bring himself to look up the history of Roman Colchester on the internet. When he did, he found the descriptions of the Iceni attack sounded clinical, tidy, almost as if they were untrue. He stared at all the pictures he could find of Boudica, but none of them struck him as real. Although he had never seen her, when he was in the Temple he had imagined her as wild, ferocious and beautiful, the rightful leader of Bereca's people.

Sometimes he couldn't stop himself thinking about Bereca. 'I'll see you in Rome,' he had said to him, and part of him longed to know if his friend had made it to Londinium, and from there to Rome.

A few weeks later, as he was changing into his football kit for a games lesson at school, he felt his mobile vibrating again. He knew it was SHARP. Quickly he put the phone in his pocket and went up to the PE teacher.

'Please, Sir, I need the loo. I can't wait – really Sir.'

'Jamie Tate – you're a pain. Hurry up, we need to pick the teams for the match.' The teacher shook his head as Jamie shot off in the direction of the toilet block, not seeing that at the last moment Jamie dodged to the right and hid behind the canteen. When Jamie flicked his phone open, the screen was swirling in the familiar blue colour, and he crouched down to wait for the message to appear.

Jamie, this is SHARP. We would like to congratulate you on your time in Roman Colchester. We have now processed all the information you collected for us and it has enabled us to fully update the records for that period. Congratulations – an impressive performance for a first time.

Jamie smiled to himself. It was good to hear that SHARP was impressed.

We would like to invite you for a second trip. At the moment we are not sure when this will be, but would you consider doing this again?

Jamie's initial reaction was sheer excitement, as if electric currents were whizzing up and down his spine. But then, for a split second, something else kicked in – was it fear? He pushed the feeling aside and, before he could change his mind, keyed in: 'Yes'.

Good, we're delighted to hear that Jamie. At the moment we're scanning our files to see what period we'd like you to investigate in your area's local history. Be patient, but try to be ready to go as soon as we contact you.

Slowly the screen faded, and Jamie was left wondering where he'd go to next. Would it be as dangerous as the last trip? He shoved his phone in his pocket and shot back to join the others on the pitch.

It was nearly two weeks before SHARP got in touch again, and although he had been waiting for it, when his phone vibrated, he very nearly fell out of a tree! He was out in the woods on his own and had decided to try and climb a tree that might give him a better view of the nesting swans at the edge of the pond. Quickly he settled himself back against the trunk of the tree, feeling its rough bark through his thin T shirt, and looked at the screen.

Hello Jamie, this is SHARP. Are you in a place where you won't be disturbed for a while?

Yes, it's OK. No one will expect me back home for ages.

Good.

Jamie wondered whether the people at SHARP were watching him at this very moment? He looked around him, half expecting to see Leika standing on the ground under the tree. Another message flashed up.

No Jamie, we can't see you right now.

Jamie was startled. Did they even know what he was thinking?

But of course we can when you are time travelling. That is essential for your safety. Can we read your thoughts? Well, I suppose it's more that we can guess them. Most people react to our messages in the same way. We may be technologically in advance of your own time, but as far as reading your mind goes, no. Whilst you're on a trip we can monitor your pulse rate and blood pressure, which gives us some idea of your emotional state and the level of danger you're being exposed to, but actual mind-reading – no, not yet.

Throughout all the excitement of time travel he hadn't really thought too much about how SHARP was keeping an eye on him, and what they knew about him. But of course it was reassuring to know that he wasn't entirely alone when he journeyed back into the past.

Right, Jamie. We have chosen your next assignment. If you are ready to proceed, key in your number 16008 and press the black phoenix.

Here are the details for your new trip. Read them several times and, as before, try to memorise them.

‹Time zone›
1884.

‹Place›
Small village to the south of Colchester.

‹Landing zone›
A barn on a small farm.

‹Instructions›
When you arrive, look in the hay stack and you will find some clothing. Put them on quickly. Remember that by doing so you will take on the character and personality of the person you will be. Leave the barn and as you walk across the farmyard someone will meet you. Go with them.

‹Identity›

They will refer to you as Sam. He is a boy who works on the farm.

‹Conditions›

Favourable at present but we are expecting a minor event to take place shortly after you arrive. Don't be alarmed — we do not anticipate that you will be in too much danger. Do you have any questions?

No, it's fine, Jamie typed in. I'm happy with what you said. I'll go when you're ready.

Excellent, Jamie. Now remember to strip off down to your underpants, put your mobile in the time/space travel bag which you will find on the branch next to you and press it tightly against your side. Press the green phoenix and key in the number 16008. Your journey will then begin. Good luck — and remember, we'll be with you all the way!

Jamie could tell that they were being really reassuring. Obviously they knew he must be a bit jumpy after last time. He slid down to the ground and took off his T shirt, trainers and trousers. He pressed the travel bag tightly against his skin, pressed the green phoenix and keyed in the numbers. As before, a high-pitched whine came nearer and nearer and then... Nothing.

CHAPTER 10

Finding The Great Great Greats At Home

This time the landing place was a pile of hay in a dark barn, which smelt strongly of cows and pigs. For a few moments, Jamie felt sick and giddy. He recognised the feeling as something that happened with time travelling. He stood up and looked about him. One end of the barn was stacked high with hay, not baled, as it would be on his dad's farm, but tied loosely into great bundles. At the far end Jamie could see animals moving quietly in their stalls, their breath hanging like mist in the still air. He looked around and found the clothes. He recognised them from old pictures of farms in the Victorian age; a thick shirt and jacket, heavy trousers and socks, and a pair of big boots that took some pulling on. Finally there was a flat cap like the one he'd seen his granddad wearing. The clothes didn't smell too fresh, but at least he knew what the smell was, cows, pigs and muck. He carefully put his mobile into the time/space travel bag and took out the silver disc, pressing it onto his forehead, the transparent film disappearing into his skin and the backing coming away. There were no hearing aids for language translation this time. He went towards the barn doors and slowly pushed them open.

He walked out into a farmyard, which had barns and pig sties built around three sides. Immediately in front of him was a house, a low red brick building with a small chestnut tree off to the right and a duck pond. Just in front of the house was a low stone trough and an old-fashioned pump with a wooden bucket hanging from the handle. A man was standing there, puffing thoughtfully on his pipe.

'Ah, there you are Sam,' called the pipe smoker, walking over towards Jamie. 'I shall be going into market today but I want you to stay behind and clean out the cow shed. Hopefully I'll get a good price for them sheep, and I might be able to buy a couple of good milking cows. We could do with some more. Now boy, go and harness up the old horse, we'll need to bring out the cart and then we can load up the sheep.'

As the man turned away, Jamie looked around quickly. Where was the stable? Ah, he could see a horse's head looking out of one of the doors opposite the big barn. There was an elderly man inside already, bent almost double with age. But his hand on the horse's neck and the low crooning sound he made to her told Jamie that he was a real old horseman.

The man looked up as Jamie went into the stable.

'There you are lad. I've harnessed up the old mare for you.' Jamie was glad about this because, although they had horses on the farm, they were for riding, and he hadn't a clue how to deal with harnessing carthorses. 'I'll lead her out if you pull out the cart and hold up the shafts.'

An old wooden wagon was parked at the side of the barn. As the horse was led out Jamie lifted up the shafts and the old man backed the mare effortlessly up to them and buckled up the traces.

'Aye lad, you know how I like the old girl,' he said to Jamie as he fondled the mare's head. 'She and I go back a long way and a finer mare you won't find anywhere else.'

For a moment he paused, his eyes staring into the distance. 'Aye, aye, a long time. But never mind an old man's talk. The master has asked me to go to market with him today, so we'll have to leave you in charge.'

'Seth, Sam,' called a voice from across the yard. 'Help me catch these sheep! Pesky things won't let me get at them.' Jamie followed Seth (obviously this was the old man's name) into a covered yard where the farmer was trying to corner four sheep. At last, thought Jamie, something I know how to do. Expertly he caught one of them and manhandled her over to the cart, where Seth and the farmer helped him to lift her in. The other three sheep followed just as easily.

'Good work, Sam,' said the farmer, as he and Seth climbed on to the cart. A woman came bustling out of the house. She was carrying a small child on her hip and handed the men a basket covered in a clean cloth. No doubt their lunch, thought Jamie.

'Thank you, my dear,' said the farmer. 'We won't be late back, and young Sam here can help you if you need anything. He'll be working near the house for most of the day.' He bent down and kissed the woman on the cheek, ruffled the little boy's hair and drove out of the yard on to the track beyond. Jamie watched, fascinated as the horse and cart clattered down the road. The woman come over to him.

'Sam,' she said, 'I have some work to do in the dairy. The little 'un can play in the yard. Just keep an eye on him for me.' She put down the child, he could only have been a couple of years old, and went into the barn at the other side of the yard. The little boy sat down on the ground and started playing with some sticks, poking them into the grounds to make a fence.

The morning wore on peacefully. Jamie was quite happy clearing out the cowshed. Cows, he thought, were beautiful creatures. They were so quiet and patient, their warm breath hanging in the air and softly blowing over you. He loved to watch them gently chewing as they pulled the hay from their manger. It was hard work clearing out the shed, but he didn't mind, and every now and then he looked out to check on the little boy, who seemed quite content to sit in the yard and play with the things he found on the ground. Once his mother came out of the dairy and gave him a cup of milk, and Jamie heard the clank of buckets as she went back to the dairy. As he worked, Jamie idly wondered why SHARP had sent him here. Everything was so peaceful. The gentle sounds of the countryside filled the air; the chiming of the church clock in the distance, the bleating of sheep out in the fields, the crowing of a cockerel, the wind softly sighing in the trees.

Then suddenly, there seemed to be a change. The cows stopped their chewing and held up their heads, and Jamie could see that their breathing had changed, as if something was about to happen. Was a storm coming? The rooks in the trees outside flew into the air in a great black cloud, screaming wildly, and the sheep in the fields stopped grazing and stood with their heads high. All the animals seemed to be on full alert, sensing danger. But it was the silence that made the hairs on Jamie's neck stand on end, the complete and utter silence which fell upon the land. No birdsong, no sound at all. It was as if someone, or something, had switched off all the noise of the countryside around him. Not a single sound.

The rumbling, when it came, at first seemed to be very far away, like the sound of a large lorry on a distant road. But it got louder and louder; now it was like an express train hurtling towards them. Jamie gripped the handle of the muck fork tightly and saw how the blood drained away from his knuckles, leaving them deathly white. The cows were moving restlessly in their stalls, their breath coming in loud snorts. And then the ground began to shake, gently at first as if a heavy wagon was passing by on the track outside, and then more fiercely until Jamie had to hang onto the door to stand upright. He heard the farmer's wife screaming, and tiles began to fall off the roof and crash to the ground in the yard. Then a crack appeared in the wall, getting wider and wider. Jamie stared at it transfixed in horror. In the distance he heard a clamour of bells coming from the village church. There was a huge crash as the building next to the cowshed collapsed into a pile of rubble, and the air was thick with dust. As the noise increased, the ground under his feet seemed to lift and drop; it felt as though someone was shaking a giant carpet. He staggered out into the yard, pulling open the door as he went. The terrified cows bolted out of the stable yard, narrowly missing the farmer's wife as she fled out of the dairy. The little boy was nowhere to be seen.

Jamie had no idea how long this chaos had lasted. It was probably only a minute or two but it seemed like eternity. The ground shook alarmingly and he ran forward, trying to avoid bricks that were falling from the buildings all around him. Gradually the rumbling faded and the ground steadied, while Jamie doubled up, coughing the dust out of his lungs. He was struggling to understand what had just happened. Surely not... surely this hadn't been an earthquake?

He was jolted back to the present by the screaming of the farmer's wife.

'Jamie!' she wailed 'Jamie, where are you?'

He rushed up to her.

'It's alright ma'am, I'm here,' he said but she looked through him as if she couldn't understand what he had said.

'Sam, where's Jamie? Where is he?'

For a moment he hesitated, and then he realised she was talking about the little boy.

'Sam, where is he?'

'I don't know – he was playing out here in the yard by the gate. Don't worry, we'll find him. He can't be far.'

But as Jamie looked round wildly at the destruction, a terrible thought came to him. The buildings on one side of the farmyard had collapsed completely, leaving a huge pile of plaster, wooden beams and bricks scattered everywhere. The pig sties, which thank goodness were empty, were partially destroyed. Despairingly, Jamie realised that if the little boy had been in any of those, he probably wouldn't have survived. But he must try to find him.

The farmer's wife was sobbing and screaming uncontrollably, saying the little boy's name over and over again.

'Ma'am,' he said, gently shaking her shoulder. 'I'll look for Jamie – I'm sure I'll find him. You go for help.' She looked at him uncomprehendingly, as if she hadn't even heard what he had said. He shook her again, more roughly this time, and at last got a reaction.

'Yes, I'll run for help. Sam, find him…oh please find him!'

As she lifted her skirts and scrambled over the piles of rubble towards the road, Jamie headed into what remained of the pig sties. The dust was beginning to settle, but loose beams swung drunkenly in the wind and he was afraid that any movement would bring them crashing down on his head. Steady, go carefully, don't rush… He began to push his way through the debris, tunnelling under the remains of the roof that had collapsed to waist height. He stopped and called out the child's name, then strained his ears to hear any noise. Again and again he called, carefully pulling bricks away to get further in.

And then he heard it, a faint whimper almost under his feet. A door had fallen against a pile of rubble and underneath it, only just visible, was the face of the child. Frantically, Jamie pulled at the door, forcing it free. He picked up the tiny boy, cradled him against his chest and ran out into the yard just as an aftershock brought the whole building down. A few seconds later and it would have been too late for both of them.

When the farmer's wife and the other villagers came running into the yard, they found him cradling the little boy in his arms. Both of them were covered in brick dust, and the little boy had a bad cut on his head, but other than that, he was none the worse. As soon as the baby saw his mother, he began to yell loudly. With tears streaming down her face she grabbed the child and kissed him over and over.

'Oh Sam, thank you. You saved my little one. I can never thank you enough.'

The men crowded round Jamie and clapped him on the back, and someone pushed a jug of ale into his hand. It tasted so good.

The sound of galloping hooves along the track announced the return of Seth and the farmer. They had just started back from Colchester when the earthquake hit and, in the confusion and the damage it had caused, it had made it difficult to make good time. In every village along the road, they later told everyone, most of the houses had been damaged in some way. Tiles had been shaken off roofs, and some buildings had collapsed completely. People spoke of how the church bells had swung violently as the ground shook, as if the devil himself was pulling all the ropes at once, and in their own village the church tower had begun to tilt and now stood at an angle. With a start, Jamie remembered that the church in his own village had a tilt. He had never really thought about why it was not straight, but now he thought he knew. And this farm – it had somehow seemed familiar to him when he arrived. Like the pieces of a jigsaw falling into place, Jamie began to see why. Much was very different, but this was his own farm, his home... SHARP had brought him back here as it was over a hundred years ago.

'We are so lucky,' the farmer said that night as they sat round the great scrubbed wooden table in the farmhouse kitchen. 'There's been a lot of damage, but so far I've only heard of one or two people losing their lives. We must thank God for saving us from this great peril.' Reaching down he gently fondled little Jamie, who was now sleeping peacefully in his mother's arms. 'We must thank God, and you too Sam, my lad. Without your bravery this little child would have died before his time. Thank you, thank you from the bottom of my heart.' Then he laughed. 'Look at that,' he pointed to the grandfather clock standing in one corner of the room. 'I certainly bought a good'un from Jeffrey's and Sons when I got that clock. It's still ticking!' Everyone laughed, and Jamie felt a lump rise in his throat; the clock that was still ticking after an earthquake, now stood in the front room of his home.

Jamie looked round at the people in the kitchen. He had only been with them a few hours, but somehow he felt so at home with them. They were good solid countrymen who, like him, loved the land and the animals who lived on it, who were outside in all weathers working in the fields and the woods, just as he did at home. But now he knew that his home was theirs too, even though so many years separated them. Old Seth sat puffing at his pipe. He looked long and hard at Jamie and smiled at him.

'Aye, you're a good lad Sam. Today you did a fine thing, saving the life of this little child. One day you will understand the importance of what you've done, but for now stick to your guns, lad. We'll make a real farmer of you yet!'

The old man turned to the farmer, and for Jamie, the last piece of the puzzle fell into place.

'You're right, Mr. Tate sir. He's a good lad.'

Mr. Tate? Mr. Tate? For a moment Jamie thought he had misheard. The farmer's name was Tate? How could it be? And if he was, that made the baby Jamie Tate – his namesake. Just at that moment, when his mind was whirling with the shock of this discovery, he felt his mobile vibrating against his side.

As soon as he could, Jamie got outside into the

farmyard. The night was cool, and he looked up into a sky spangled with thousands of stars. Over in the cowshed the new beasts were eating their hay, and compared with the chaos of a few hours earlier, the scene was incredibly peaceful. Jamie took his mobile out and looked at the screen. There was a message from SHARP.

Well done Jamie. We have all the information we need about the occurrence of the Essex Earthquake. Your first trip back to Roman Colchester told us about an event of great historical importance, but SHARP is interested in smaller events as well. Everything adds to the knowledge of humankind.

The screen slowly faded and Jamie thought the message was over, but then another one flashed up, this time from Leika.

Well done Jamie! I hope you enjoyed your trip, and returning you back shouldn't present any difficulties this time.

Quickly Jamie sent a text message in reply: You knew, didn't you?

Knew what, Jamie?

That you were sending me back in time to my own home – to the farm as it was in Victorian times. There was a pause, and then another message flashed up.

Yes, of course we knew. Perhaps I'm out of order to tell you this Jamie, but if you work hard at school, one day you will make a huge difference to this place, this countryside, this country. Remember that, and don't let anyone put you off working towards what you really want in life.

Again the screen faded and the darkness of the night closed around him. An owl hooted in the nearby tree, far away a vixen called, and the warm breath of the cows hung in the air.

Another message flashed up – SHARP again.

Jamie, we're now ready to bring you back to your own time. Remember, go into the cowshed, take off all your clothes except your shorts and leave them neatly on the hay. By doing this you will become yourself again and leave Sam in his own time. When you're ready dial 16008 and press the red phoenix. And don't worry – our transporter is working well and there should be no problems bringing you back this time.

Quietly, Jamie went to the cowshed. For a moment he stood fondling the animals' ears, talking to them softly in the light of the old oil lamp. It was weird to think that in a moment or two all of this would be part of history, that these gentle animals and the people in the farmhouse would have been dead for over a hundred years.

He pressed the red phoenix and the bright night sky whirled around him. Coming towards him was a sound that he recognised very well now, a high-pitched whine and then...Nothing.

That night as the family sat round the big wooden table in the kitchen, Jamie thought of another family who had done the same all those years ago. He couldn't help wondering if any of his family knew about the earthquake that had so nearly caused the family not to exist. Almost casually he turned to his dad.

'What do you know about the Essex Earthquake,

Dad?' he asked.

'Essex Earthquake? Why do you want to know about that?' asked in his gran.

'Oh, I need to find out about it for school,' Jamie replied.

The three adults looked at each other with raised eyebrows. What's got into Jamie? they wondered. Why is he so keen about school all of a sudden?

'Well,' said Mr. Tate. 'I know a bit – read a book about it a few years ago. It was in the 1880s I think, and the centre of the earthquake was in this area. Caused quite a lot of damage, but I don't know if anyone was actually killed or not.'

'Now then,' said Gran, who regularly went to the services at the village church, 'I do know that the shaking of the ground made the church tower lean slightly over to one side, and it has stayed there ever since. Must have been quite something.'

'Oh it was' said Jamie, without thinking, but quickly changed what he was about to say when he saw the look on everyone's faces. 'Yes, it was in the 1880s. Dad's right, my teacher told us.'

The following evening after school, Gran and Jamie walked down to the village church. It was quite an impressive building, but what made it more remarkable was its tower, which had a definite lean to one side. Jamie had never really thought about why it was like that, but then he remembered – as vividly as if it was happening all over again – the ground moving under his feet like a rough sea and the clanging of church bells in the distance. Jamie's gran went inside while Jamie wondered round the graveyard.

'Jamie!' Gran called out. 'Oh there you are. Come inside and look. I've found the book.'

Someone had taken a lot of trouble to cut out articles from a local newspaper and stick them into a scrapbook. The pages were yellow with age and the ink faded, but there it all was; a description of the earthquake and one or two quaint old pictures of solemn looking people in Victorian clothes standing around houses which had collapsed into heaps of rubble. And here, finally, was what Jamie wanted to see: a short paragraph about how a little boy had been rescued by one of the farm workers after a barn had collapsed on him. The rescuer's name was given as Sam Williams, and the child's as Jamie Tate, the farmer's son, aged two. Jamie had saved his own great-great-grand dad!

Later that evening, Jamie walked out to the pond, the same one where he'd first seen Leika and heard about SHARP. So many things had happened since then, and he had learnt so much. As he lay at the edge of the pool and stared into the water, Jamie saw images of what had happened; Bereca, sitting in the dark and trying to tell him how he felt about the tribes' revolt, the clasp of his hand on Bereca's, the blood curdling cries of the Iceni as they attacked the Temple, and the look on Flavius's face when he had said 'Now Marcus, now is the time – you cannot change what will happen.' Although SHARP had dulled the pain of those memories, Jamie knew he would never forget them. And then he thought of the farmer and his wife, old Seth and little Jamie; the way the ground had shook and moved, and the sound of the distant bells. He couldn't change the past, but he could do something about the future. Of all the things that had happened to him, that was the most important thing he had learnt, he could change the future if he tried.

Smiling to himself, Jamie called Doodles to his side and together they walked back through the fields to the farmhouse.

Collect the other exciting books in the Time Traveller Kids series and discover the history of famous sites in the United Kingdom

Danny's interest in history is zero, but when a mysterious boy, claiming to be from a future organisation called SHARP gets in contact with him on his mobile, Danny agrees to travel back to the Tudor period. Making friends in the long-forgotten past gets him seriously hooked on time travel, not to mention history!

Danny has become an experienced time traveller but this doesn't help him when SHARP's communication systems fail. It is the year 671, the Dark Ages and he is left stranded in the depths of winter when wolves roamed the English countryside and Danny cannot understand a word the strange people speak.

Incredibly musically gifted, Atlanta is entranced by the music of the far-into-the- future humankind. Is this what makes her agree to join the growing band of twenty first century kids who go back in time to gather information for the organisation called SHARP?

When Alex McLean is catapulted back to 1314 by a rival outfit to SHARP, his life is in serious danger. This organisation, called STRAP, do not care if he falls to his death when he joins the desperate band of Scots fighters who did the impossible and scaled the terrifying Rock on which Edinburgh Castle stands to this day.

Jo Kelly's parents, both Oxford Academics, are so busy fussing over her super bright brother, who is a chorister in the world famous Magdalen College choir, that they don't realize they are ignoring Jo. How envious they would be, if they knew that Jo is sent back in time to Oxford 1939 and that she actually meets the legendary C.S. Lewis and J.R. Tolkien.

When ten-year-old Sarah accepts the challenge to travel back in time, she thought that she might meet Robin Hood. She had not bargained on joining a band of half-starved children toiling deep under ground in a south Yorkshire coalmine. She becomes a 'trapper' – a child who pulled a string to open a trap to let the trucks of coal hurtle onwards down the tunnel, that is until the mine started flooding. Sarah's life is in danger!

Competitions And Activities

Seven Arches Publishing often runs competitions for you to enter with prizes of book tokens, that can be spent in any bookshop, for solving puzzles or for a good illustration. Why not go to www.sevenarches-publishing.co.uk and check out whether there is competition or activity on its way based on one or other of our books. We often include the winning entries of our competitions, or the writing, poems or pictures that you send us in the next print run of the title.

Contact Us

You are welcome to contact Seven Arches Publishing by:

Phone: 0161 4257642

Or

Email: admin@sevenarchespublishing.co.uk